MW01602703

Tales from "Prickly Path"

**A Collection of Original Short Stories,
Fact, Half-Truth and Just Plain Old Fabrication**

Tales from "Prickly Path"

**A Collection of Original Short Stories,
Fact, Half-Truth and Just Plain Old Fabrication**

Don Lee

This book is dedicated to my family, friends, and the Lord, for the life experiences they have given me.

Contents

Prologue   XI

Editor's Note   XIII

About the Author   XV

Losing Judy   3   *[Charlotte]*
My struggle with the death of my wife of thirty-three years.

Two Tough Horned Frogs   9
The Hoits. There are no bigger fans of Texas Christian University football.

Three Special Friends   12   *[Broker MBL]*
Born again and spreading the word.

Ben's Last Address   19   *[Jim Corah]*
A call to action by the master.

Smoking, Inside the Box   23   *[Parris Isl 66]*
Some people will do anything for a cigarette.

Lady of Chinju   27   *[S. Korea]*
Based on a true story of honor.

Culinary Adventures with Norman   31
There is only one Norman. God love him.

It Was The Best Time!   35
Lots of gin & tonic and lots of laughs.

Test Procedure Step 97   39
A motive, a killer, a robot, and a computer.

Tales from West Island   42
Some fun stories about my college days with Pete.

Thank You ...   46
You never know who will come to your aid when the chips are down.

The Hill   50
Some fun stories about days on Beacon Hill in Boston.

Last in the Line to Farm   62
The warm story of life on a farm.

The Powerful Force   66
Brut force meets a different powerful force.

The Right Coach   71
I wish Coach Thomas had been my coach in High School.

The Rush Project   75
What is going on here? ... surprise!

The Secret   80
For the love of your neighbor.

Three Oranges   85
Some things are not always as they seem.

Truly, the Best of Friends   89
My description of a true story of friendship.

Two Days in Hell   93
The reality of war.

Exodus   98
An exodus by any other name is still an Exodus.

Flying Death   101
Better know who your friends are.

Charlotte's Wish   104
A Christmas wish comes true.

Guests of John and Mable   109
A whimsical tale set at the Ringling Museum, Sarasota, Florida.

LAX Gate 68C   116
A gate that only certain people may see.

Lost   120
The evil Captain Ismis meets his watery demise.

MISSION X4123   124
A very boring situation is bearable if you have a good book.

Three TV's   128
Three fun TV stories.

Oh No, Not Again   133
A very valuable coincidence.

Otis and Wally   137
A story of friendship.

Premonition   142
A story based on the customs of the Wampanoag Indians.

Singing Birds   146
A bitter snowstorm, but the birds will always sing.

Texas Justice   151
Don't mess with Texas.

That Exhilarating Feeling   155
Better keep your eye on the ball.

The Ladies of the Mission   159
A story of two ladies who work tirelessly for the mission.

The Man from D Block   162
Sometimes miserable people may surprise you.

The Road Trip   166
A father and son story made possible by a tragic event.

They Were All There   170
A story about family and friends who celebrate our special events.

When Woody Met Meg   174
This one is dedicated to you, Woody.

Walking with Jesus   178
The Disciples learn about Jesus, Heaven, and Hell.

Acknowledgments   182

Prologue

This book is a hodgepodge of stories, written over the last several years while I have traveled. A "hodgepodge" is exactly what the short story marketing people tell one not to write. I write what comes into my thoughts, so that's the way it is. I hope you will laugh, cry, be surprised, shocked, and feel joyful. It is my hope you will experience a roller coaster of emotions.

These stories span 455 AD to the year 4123. My stories are quite short which suits my attention span and I hope yours. I take you many places and I hope you enjoy the trip.

It was enjoyable writing this book and it does not matter if I sell many of the books. I'll have a copy to sit on my coffee table. Most importantly, fond memories will always lie there.

The "Prickly Path" shown on my book cover, is actually from a painting I completed about twenty years ago. The oil painting is an original copy of "Cactus in Bloom" by Porfirio Salinas. His original was 10" x 12.5". I composed my painting 48" x 48". I had a big wall to fill and I wanted the cactus field to burst with color.

Please send questions, comments, and corrections to me at tfpp.stories@gmail.com.

Editor's Note

Don Lee's voice is the power behind the words on this "Prickly Path." As an Editor, I am faced with the challenge, a challenge I do not take lightly, of retaining the writer's voice while editing the work in front of me. Read this book with your heart. It is, most certainly, a Minuet. It ebbs and flows lyrically and moves the reader's soul. It is a piece written with heart and begs to be read with heart. Enjoy your walk down the Prickly Path!

—Nancy Washburn, Editor

About the Author

I graduated from Southeastern Massachusetts University (SMU) in 1973 with a BS in Mechanical Engineering Technology. The university later became the University of Massachusetts-Dartmouth (UMD). I have pretty much stayed the same.

My work, as an engineering contractor, has taken me to eighteen states, several states multiple times, and South Korea. I recently slowed down and started writing.

A short time ago I published my first book, *Professional Contract Employment*, directed to anyone who is interested

xv

in contracting work. This book is packed with tips and really, anyone who is looking for any job or already working would benefit from reading it. You may have seen my book right at the top of the *New York Times* Least Seller's List.

I polished up my current book, *Tales from Prickly Path*, at my lake house in Western New York. I hope you enjoy reading my book as much as I enjoyed writing it.

Both books are available on my website: www.triremestudios.com

THE STORIES

Losing Judy

My struggle with the death of my wife of thirty-three years.

ON A WARM SUMMER NIGHT IN BOSTON IN 1977, I WALKED into an up-scale hotel on Commonwealth Avenue. I had never been there before, but soon found the lounge that extended out around the pool and a jubilant crowd swaying with the band. Out of a sea of faces, adjacent to the pool, and off in the distance, was a bright smile and beautiful large brown eyes. She was lovely, and I was immediately taken by her.

As the band started playing a slow song, I started winding past the myriad of obstacles of tables and seated patrons to ask her to dance.

"Excuse me, pardon me, excuse me, sorry ..."

As I got near her table, someone pushed back their chair to get up and almost sent me into the pool. I glanced at my potential dance partner and she was snickering, batting those brown eyes. I said to myself, "If she says no it will be an even longer walk back."

"Would you like to dance, miss?"

"Why yes, thank you."

As we danced, it just felt right, and right, and right again. We danced the night away and we both knew there was something special in our meeting. We were inseparable from then on and we were married not long after. In the years that followed our sons, Donald and Andy, were born.

Sharing my life with Judy was a gift. She was a wonderful friend, wife, homemaker, and mother. One of her best traits was that she was perky and excitable. She carried these traits with her and brightened up even the drabbest room. When we went out socially both men and women would be drawn to Judy's warmth. By the end of the night, many women would ask Judy to have lunch or go shopping with them. Judy was such a good listener and supportive of anyone who sought her council.

She had a wonderful hardy laugh, and laughed often, even at herself. She loved and respected all people, especially the elderly. She loved animals, birds, bugs, and especially our dogs, Bessie, Peanut, and Baxter. She took them for a walk every chance she got. Judy enjoyed golf and fishing, and yes, she baited her own hook. Judy made everything special. She always put 110% into everything she did.

She loved cooking and often spent most of the day in the kitchen. She went all out on holidays. One New Year's, she made a full Chinese dinner from scratch including wonton soup, egg rolls, sushi, saffron rice, lemon chicken stir fry, and wrote a hand written love note to me that she baked inside my fortune cookie. Our house was so scary at Halloween that those who came to trick or treat approached cautiously. At Christmas we loved to sit in the living room, within the candle glow, and enjoy the colorful lighted decorations and her Santa Claus collection.

Once the kids were out of high school, Judy obtained an Associates Degree in Drafting and Design. After several years of working, and additional class study, she was accepted to nursing school. By then, the kids were in college and we were all so happy.

About a year before Judy's first nursing fall semester, she informed me that her recent mammogram had revealed a tumor. It was an anxious week or so culminating in bad news. Judy was diagnosed with Stage 2B Breast Cancer. The tumor originated against her rib cage, under the muscle, and went undetected. At that time, this stage of cancer was associated with a 67% survivability rate. Judy felt good with this percentage and I did nothing but feed her optimism. She had a partial mastectomy, radiation, and extensive chemotherapy. Subsequent scans were clear.

Judy started nursing school and was doing well. Late in the semester she developed a sore right shoulder that we thought was caused by the strap from her heavy book sack. Her next scheduled scan revealed several tumors on her spine. Her diagnosis was Stage IV, terminal cancer. We were devastated and Judy was forced to leave school and plunge into years of treatment.

We were given about five years and we made the best of it. Judy was on continuous chemotherapy with only one ten-day break in the five years of treatment that followed. She displayed so much courage. She seldom even talked about her condition and maintained she would not die.

While Judy did not talk often about her relationship with God, there is no doubt that it was rock solid. I was with her the day she was saved. Judy had *fall back* faith. That is, she felt that when her time came, she could fall backwards, and Jesus would be there to catch her.

Of course, we all supported her and we fought all the way with her. Her last six months with us she began to slow down noticeably and the last month she was becoming frail. We seldom talked about her disease. She always felt she would prevail and the family fully supported her.

She was hospitalized for weeks late into her treatment and was very weak. I often had to carry her to the bathroom because the staff, when summoned, took so long to come to our room. One day, after I had struggled to get her to the bathroom and back to her bed, she sobbed:

"Don, thank you for being with me through all of this. I love you dearly."

This was the only time she had said anything like this to me. It was a rich reward for all that I had done for her during her years of treatment. Perhaps this explains why Jesus asks us to acknowledge his love and sacrifice from us just once. Judy died with me at her side on a chilly morning in October 2011.

Two soldiers faced off in a battle to the death. The soldier that prevailed lost and perished. The soldier that lost won ... gently falling backwards into the loving arms of Jesus.

With her death, everything we had and will ever have together died with her. You see, the whole was taken. It is this void, an insatiable pit of loss that lingers, and I fear will always linger. Opening the door to a quiet house, dinner alone, and watching TV alone would be my new life.

After a year and a half or so I perked up some and tried to get myself out there. I'd do fine until something I heard or saw reminded me of Judy and I just would go home. I went on a cruise to cheer myself up. One night, as I stood on the top aft deck of a ship looking back at the foaming wake, I realized no amount of nautical miles could lesson my emptiness.

Of course I've gone through many emotions. Did we do as much as we could? What could we have done differently? Should we have had even more medical opinions? Should we have changed doctors? Why did God do this to Judy and why did God leave me to live without her?

My faith was rocked to the core by Judy's death. But my bedrock was deep. After much soul searching and asking God to lead me out of my grief, a new path in life has been revealed to me. The grief I was carrying on my shoulders has been replaced by loving, happy memories tucked away in a special place in my heart. I am so thankful having known her and our thirty-three years of marriage. While she is not at my side, I am not alone.

It occurred to me that from the day we got married, one of us would have to face life without each other. I am glad it is me.

Now, after almost four years, I walk tall with my shoulders square along a lighted path and look forward to what awaits me around the next bend. I hope those I pass feel God's love in me and know that his love is freely given to them. The Lord has taken much, but given much more.

Epilogue

Long before our grandchildren were born, Judy talked about passing along her lessons of life to our grandchildren if we were lucky enough to have them. Judy talked often about her life and what was important to her. In 2011, my youngest son, Andy, and his wife Jana, gave us little Charlotte. Judy adored Charlotte. When Charlotte was still very young Judy's cancer began to take a toll on her and she died without being able to talk with Charlotte. A year after Judy passed away little Oliver was born to

Jana and Andy. I'm sure Judy would have passed similar thoughts to Oliver.

The following letter, written by Grampy, is a letter to our grandchildren from their loving Grandmother, Nana.

Dear Charlotte,

I love you dearly and will always love you. When I held you in my arms and looked into your eyes I saw myself as a child and I was overcome with the wonderful thoughts about all the good things coming in your life. My dear Charlotte, I cannot be with you as you flower into a young lady. Before your first birthday, I became very ill and the Lord called me home.

There are some important thoughts I would like to share with you:

Be a good listener, a loyal friend, and treat all people and God's creatures with respect. Thank God often for the blessings in your life.

Plan ahead, always have a fun activity in the future to look forward to. Obtain a solid education to allow yourself to be independent. Live life on your terms.

Follow your dreams. As you look to improve yourself and your lot in life, never let anyone tell you that you cannot do something. Always put 100% into everything you do. Keep moving forward, and never, never, quit.

Charlotte, please carry this letter with you as you go through life. In the still of the night talk with me often. I will always be there and I am a very good listener.

With all my love,

Nana

Two Tough Horned Frogs

*The Hoits. There are no bigger fans of Texas
Christian University football.*

THE HORNED FROG HAS LONG BEEN THE OFFICIAL MASCOT OF *Texas Christian University. In 1992 the state legislature of Texas passed a law establishing the Horned Toad (aka Horned Frog) as the official state reptile.*

The purple and white ran deep, deep into the souls of Jack and Marion Hoit, Texas Christian University Horned Frog football fans for sixty-two years.

Marion Davis was brought up right down the street from Amon Carter Stadium, the home of the Texas Christian University football Horned Frogs. Her dad, a loyal fan, was confined to a wheelchair. He listened to the games on his radio and always had his window open to hear the roar of the crowd when the Frogs scored. Marion loved TCU also and had accomplished her dream of studying Art at TCU.

Jack Hoit had recently moved to Fort Worth, Texas to work in a foundry in January 1947. He had always loved football, but since he had recently moved to town he had no local team to follow. He was hundreds of miles from his beloved Thomas High 'Wild Turkeys.' That football void would be filled soon after a day in the local Arboretum.

I remember the first time I saw them walk by, climbing the steep concrete stadium steps to their seats that they had reserved for forty-three years. They were elderly then, holding hands, and always very nicely dressed. Jack always wore gray slacks, white shirt, light purple tie, dark purple sweater, and a Horned Frog ball cap. Marion, always wore a white blouse, purple skirt, and was bathed in Horned Frog accessories. When they walked up the steps, everyone would look at them and feel their spirit! That wonderful warm school spirit!

The sun was pouring down on the Arboretum that late March day in 1948. Jack loved cactus and the Arboretum had a dandy of a cactus garden. As Jack was bending over looking at a cactus bloom, Marion Davis, a lovely, TCU co-ed bumped into him.

"Oh, I'm so sorry, sir."

"Oh, that's OK. It's a good thing I didn't fall into all those thorns. I love cactus though."

"Wow! I'm an Art major at TCU and I'm here to paint the cactus garden. I love cactus also."

Jack and Marion dated and soon the cactus blooms aligned. Following Marion's graduation, they were married. They were fixtures at all the home football games. Also, in the early days, they went to as many away games as they could. As the years rolled by, I would always see them walking, albeit a little slower each year, up the steps, way up, beyond our seats.

Jack had a distinctive voice. When he yelled out "Go Frogs," I'm sure even some of the players on the other side of the field heard him. I remember one night game in late November, the frigid winds had driven even the most loyal fans out of the stands, but there they were, the Hoits, all bundled up in an igloo of blankets.

Jack had a tough go of it in his later years. He had heart bypass surgery, several mini-strokes, and three major strokes that left him barely able to walk or talk. But, walk he did. I don't believe either one of them ever missed a home football game.

One cool October day, a few years later, the Frogs faced New Mexico. 'The Lobo's' always gave it a good go against us. The Hoit's, now in their eighties, walked by us, slowly, up the steps. About a minute later, we heard a lot of commotion behind us. Just as we turned, Marion rolled by us on the steep steps, screaming. She had fallen backwards on the steps, and rolled about fifty feet bouncing between the metal handrail and seated fans. She looked like a rag doll being tossed in the fall. Several fans attempted to break her fall but could not. She came to rest against a concrete wall at the base of the steps. She had bounced down thirty rows of seats!

Incredibly, the time-tested Lady Horned Frog stood up and brushed herself off. By then, Jack had made it down to the base of the stairs to assist her. As an ovation ensued, they faced the crowd and gave the Horned Frog hand sign and began slowly ascending the steps back up to their seats. In all my years at the stadium, I had never heard such a roar from the crowd. It's a wonder how she could take a fall like that and not have major injuries. She and Jack were two tough Horned Frogs.

Three Special Friends

Born again and spreading the word.

Mr. Phillips, you must come down and pick-up your Rolex. We completed the repair weeks ago. This is the third time we have reached out to you. If you don't pay for the repair by Friday we will take possession of the watch, based on the repair agreement."

"Mr. Phillips, when will you be paying your rent?"

"We have not heard from you in weeks, sir, you really must pay us the minimum on you credit card."

Randy Phillips was in a position most of us have been in at least one time in our life. He was overextended, and knew it. However, this time climbing out of it would prove difficult.

Bill, Randy's boss, approaches Randy one day at work:

"Randy, you seem to be receiving a lot of calls at work. I need you to spend your time assisting our clients and increasing your sales. Your sales numbers are not keeping up."

"I'm sorry, Bill. I'll pick up the pace."

Randy had been working for a stock brokerage company in New York City for some time. He had been a top performer. However, of late, was struggling with the sales demands placed upon the staff. He had a beautiful apartment in the city overlooking Washington Square and an active social life. However, he often was nursing a splitting headache from his pressure cooker job. He felt he was invincible, as did his two best friends, Johnny and Chris. They all were affluent, and they all worked hard and played hard. Just keep working through this he would often tell himself.

"Chris, I'm thinking of moving. I need to live within my means."

"Come on, Randy, you have a great apartment and job. Relax, the money is good and will always be there.

"Chris, you don't seem to understand. I can't meet my debts."

"So does this mean that you won't be able to hang with Johnny and me?" asked Chris.

A few weeks later at work:

"Randy, would you come into my office?" said Bill. As Randy walked into Bill's office, he was alarmed to see Wayne, the office manager, seated.

"Sit down, Randy." Bill offered. "Randy, as you may be aware, conditions are difficult in our industry. When things slow down, people have less to invest. We need to let you go, Randy. Your last day will be next Friday. We're prepared to pay you a month's severance pay. Good luck to you in the future."

"But Bill, I need this job, I'm not in position to lose my job."

"I'm sorry Randy, most people aren't, I'm very sorry. Your accounts will be given to William. Please get with him to discuss theses accounts."

Randy was devastated. Now he has no job and is in debt. He starts thinking about options: all not good. One thing is for certain, his view of Washington Square is history.

"Hey Randy, what's this we hear about you getting the ax?" asked Johnny.

"Who did you hear that from, Johnny?"

"Chris."

"Yeah, my last day is this Friday.

"This Friday! I'd say we'd go out after work, but I've got a hot date on Friday. Don't worry Randy, there's lots of work out there."

"I wish, Johnny. Actually, I've been looking for months to get into a better job situation. There's nothing out there with business conditions as such."

Randy returns to his desk and takes a call from the company from which he has rented his apartment furniture:

"Mr. Phillips, will you be home around 2p.m. tomorrow? I'm sorry, but we must repossess your furniture."

Randy winced, and answered under duress, "Yes, I'll meet you there at 2p.m."

Randy never thought his world of gorgeous apartments, clubs, restaurants, and his circle of beautiful friends living the good life would end. Now, the end was in sight.

Randy meets Chris and Johnny down in the break room:

"Guys … I'm in a jam. I have to move out of my apartment. I'm going to a boarding house."

"A boarding house!" said Chris. "Come on man, things can't be that bad."

"I need to cut back, way back. Would you guys help me move?"

"Randy, I'd offer to have you to stay with me for awhile, but, it would really cramp my style," said Chris.

"Yeah, same here," said Johnny. "I guess we could help you move though."

Randy arranged for a room in a boarding house in as best an area of town as possible. No matter what date and time Randy proposed to move, Chris and Johnny were always busy. He called his girlfriend, Karen, several times to ask her to help him, but ever since he told her he was let go, she did not return his calls. Willy, a guy on the first floor of the boarding house, offered to help Randy. The move took all day and they both were exhausted.

His room came with one chair, a bed, and one window ... with a view of an alleyway. As Randy rested in the chair, he looked out the window across all the packed boxes. Gone was the view of Washington Square replaced by a cracked brick wall. As the sun lowered and the alleyway dimmed, he was very anxious about his future. Life would be different for Randy, but he decided he would not be a victim. He would build his life back up.

Willy introduced Randy to the owner of a local grocery store. The owner offered Randy a job stocking and maintaining the produce section. Soon, Randy found pride in displaying and maintaining the produce. He loved the smells, especially, the limes and bananas. He often found enjoyment talking with the customers and helping them with their produce purchases.

"Hey, Randy. I'm having a few friends over on Sunday. Actually, we meet every Sunday. Would you like to join us?" asked Willy.

"Are you having a party, Willy?"

"Well ... sort of. We all sit around out back of the building in the small courtyard and talk, mainly about Our Father. Please bring the chair from your room. There's just grass out there."

"So, these are all family members?" Randy asked.

"Actually, only Jill and Jana, the two sisters from 203 are related."

"Oh ... OK, what time?"

"Two o'clock is good. See you there."

"Great, I'll bring some fresh fruit from the store."

Randy was making progress on his debt, even with his drastically reduced salary. He had fresh flowers and a big bowl of fresh fruit in his room. He had not seen Johnny or Chris in weeks and that was fine with him. He looked forward to Sunday.

Before he knew it the backyard was full of people.

"Hi, my name is Nancy."

"Hi, Nancy. My name is Randy."

"Randy, we are all happy that you have joined us today. We know, like us, you will feel closer to Our Father and fulfillment."

Throughout the afternoon various people shared the religious experiences they had during the week. Randy could only listen intently. He was moved by the glowing stories and the sense of joy in their voices. It didn't hurt that he thought that Nancy was cute.

Soon the big day came ... financial freedom. He was debt free! He marveled that given his simple life, he was so happy. He had been seeing Nancy and when he looked into her eyes he saw warmth that no other woman had ever portrayed. He was attending the groups' meetings every Sunday and wanted to learn more. Randy began to learn what faith was all about.

"Randy, faith has to be built. It's not something that you can acquire right from the start." Nancy said. "First, you must learn to know the Father and his Son. You must understand the sacrifice they both made and for whom they sacrificed. When you understand their sacrifice you will begin to build faith. Faith evolves from belief."

Randy continued to attend the meetings. It made sense to him that our world was created for us to have infinite possibilities. We were given earthly dominion and a responsibility. He learned how man was sinful and the Father, God, sent many messengers to ask us to turn away from sin. He began to realize how the Father must have agonized over, as a last resort, sending his son to ask us to turn from sin. Jesus asks us to realize that he died for our sins and to accept him as our Personal Savior. Randy reasoned that asking Jesus to be his Personal Savior and forgive his sins would open the door of Heaven.

Randy realized, like others in his group, his current good fortunes were blessings from The Father, The Son, and The Holy Ghost. Now, at night, he had someone to thank for the positive things in his life. He also found that questions he asked in the quiet of the night were answered. The big picture that he never saw out his window overlooking Washington Square could be seen anytime, anywhere. When he said the Lord's Prayer at night he felt a calm. A calm like never before.

"Randy, would you move that spinach display over on the corner?" asked the grocery store owner.

"Sure," said Randy.

As Randy turned with the first load of spinach he noticed one of his old co-workers, Chris, was looking at lettuce.

"Hello, Chris, long time no see."

Chris turned, "Randy, is that you? Man, what are you doing working in a place like this? Wow ... I never thought things would be this bad for you. Hey, Bill has been looking for you. He wants you to come back to the office. We're making money hand over fist with the new commission structure."

"Chris, this *is* my office, an office in which I feel very comfortable. I've met some nice people and made three special friends. I would like you to get to know them. They think big, really big. Would you and Johnny like to come over this Sunday?"

Ben's Last Address

A call to action by the master.

DOCTOR CORAH, PLEASE COME OVER. I THINK WE MAY have a breakthrough. We have a marked improvement in subject's skin pigment and texture, a pulse approaching the independent range, and increased muscle movement."

"Great, Professor, I'll be right over."

The year is 2164. After years of research, the scientific community is on the threshold of the ability to regenerate life. While turning the clock back is not achievable, regeneration of life appears promising. The process is lengthy, involving extensive manipulation of DNA, and extensive medical oversight.

A committee was formed to determine which deceased individual would be chosen to attempt the first regeneration.

Of the many suitable candidates reviewed, the committee just had to choose Ben Franklin.

Four years later:
"Mr. Franklin, can you hear me? Sir, this is Doctor Tim Corah. Can you hear me?"

Ben lying still, began rubbing his eyes, then slowing opened them, blinking repeatedly.

"Mr. Franklin, my name is Doctor Corah. We need to know. Can you hear me?"

"Yes, I can, sir. I am very tired and confused, I ..."

"Thank you, Mr. Franklin, you need your rest."

In the months that followed, Ben's strength began to come back slowly and he did well in both physical and social transition therapy. After some months, he began short sessions of social interaction and soon was making public appearances. The medical community was also treating the underlying conditions that originally had led to his passing.

As you may imagine, the sight of Mr. Franklin, dressed in period clothing, was an overwhelming vision. He was requested everywhere for an appearance. After touring major cities, visiting manufacturing plants, hospitals, parks, and zoos, he asked to go to less fortunate areas of various cities. He visited shelters for women and the homeless, as well as other facilities for the less fortunate. He began dressing in current dress to blend in. He spent most of his time in libraries reading about what had happened in history since his passing. In addition, he liked just sitting in the park talking with people and feeding the pigeons.

After some time he was asked to speak to a conference of scientists, doctors, and engineers. He praised them for their advances in medicine and science. He spoke of his amazement of technology that has made life much better.

Shortly after that engagement he was asked to speak before Congress. The President introduced Mr. Franklin as a brilliant innovator, inventor, and public servant.

"Mr. President, members of Congress, distinguished guests, and all Americans. Thank you for this extraordinary opportunity. I spoke recently to The Conference of Scientists, Doctors, and Engineers. I praised them for their amazing accomplishments in science, engineering, and medicine. Life today has been greatly improved by their collective efforts."

"Unfortunately, I cannot extend praise of this nature to this body, nor any such prior body in the modern era. You see, it is evident to me that today's vision of government is *for* government, not *for* the people. The people's trust has been violated wholesale, and for a long time."

"I have studied the modern history of the United States since the colonial days. It appears to me that our society has fallen into mediocrity. We are a nation that cannot look itself in the mirror."

"In my day, we had similar problems. Our issues were mostly localized. We were able to resolve them because it was for the common good. I fully understand today's problems are more difficult because they are not only local, but also regional, national, and global. But, this does not excuse this body from its duty."

"Gentlemen, our country has serious problems. I believe your first duty is to secure the nation's borders and create a pathway to citizenship for those who love this country. We must review all matters associated with national security."

"Following this, the next strength of this nation will come from rebuilding the American family and our educational system. There are countries I've never heard of with better educational systems! I heard on the television today that our children are tired in class because school starts too early. Let's face the real problem. Parents, roll up your sleeves, work with your children. Don't allow them to stay up until all hours of the night. I tell you, respect and reinforcement of work ethic will lead to children who take pride in themselves, and their studies."

"Finally, in my day, there were no handouts. Those of you in Congress, work together to build programs for the common good to educate the underclass so that they may be qualified for work. Those who are truly incapacitated must be helped. But all able bodied citizens should work. Do not deprive someone of the pride of a hard day's work, and the satisfaction of providing for their families.

"Ladies and Gentlemen: We must restore accountability and honor. Now, let's get down to work."

Mr. Franklin received a standing ovation.

In the months that followed Ben spent many hours in the park feeding the pigeons just like he had done hundreds of years ago. Some things never change he thought. Soon thereafter he passed away.

Smoking, Inside the Box

Some people will do anything for a cigarette.

THE MARINES ARE LOOKING FOR A FEW GOOD MEN. THEY didn't have that slogan when I joined up, but they got a good man back then anyway.

In the early spring of 1966 life on Beacon Hill in Boston was at it's hippie best. We partied aplenty. That is, until my draft notice came! Funny how fast your party experience ends when a letter like that is opened.

Earlier in the Spring I had been accepted to college to study engineering. I had been looking forward to my first semester and was excited about this opportunity. Struggling through a muddy rice patty in Vietnam, carrying 120 pounds of stuff, all hot and sweaty was not my idea of partying, to say nothing about people shooting at me. I was drafted into the Army and my orders stated my reporting date in sixty days. My acceptance in college was not considered a deferment at that time so now I was stuck. I soon found out that I could sign up in any of the services as long as my service commitment was met.

I looked into all the various reserve services and found that only the Marine Corps Reserve was available. I signed up as quickly as I could. My buddy, Kenny McAuley, in a similar situation as I, also signed up. Our parties on Beacon Hill would be ending soon. Too soon.

We reported in mid-August to the Marine Recruit Training Depot in Parris Island, South Carolina. We quickly learned that this island was the high humidity capital of the universe. We also found that everyone on the island who is not a recruit shouts instead of talking. Basically, we were in for sweating profusely and being constantly yelled at. It must be in the Marine Corps handbook that each sentence must contain a minimum of six swear words. Both Kenny and I smoked and we found that we would not be smoking very much while in recruit training.

When I was in high school I used to steal cigarettes from my Dad's wall dispenser. He (and I) smoked Chesterfield Regulars, a really strong smoke. I loved smoking. It was a part of my personality and look. I smoked at least two packs a day. Once on the island, on a good day, we were allowed one cigarette in the morning and one at night. Usually, we only got one. When our DI (Drill Instructor) yelled out "Smokers, go!" those that smoked rushed out of the squad bay into an open grassy area adjacent to our building. We formed a circle, arm's length circling a pail of water. Then, we stood at attention until the DI leaned out of the squad bay and yelled "Light em up." We were not allowed to talk and every time we needed to flick an ash we had to walk to the center of the circle and flick the ash into the pail. We rarely got to finish a cigarette before he yelled, "Put em out." Then we had to field strip our butts.

One day toward the end of our sweaty eight-week "vacation" on the island, we were given tear gas training. We were given a lecture concerning the deployment, adjustment, and care and cleaning of a gas mask. In front of our bleachers was a small wooden gas chamber building with closed windows way at the top.

After the lecture, they passed out gas masks and we practiced taking them out of the keeper, putting on the mask, adjusting the mask, then returning them to the keeper. We then went into the gas chamber and were told to deploy the masks. Then the instructor fired a canister of gas. Immediately, we began to feel the burning of the gas on our exposed skin. After a few minutes, the chamber door was opened. We hurried out, and cleared and returned the masks to their keepers.

Then, we re-entered the chamber. The instructor locked the door and fired a canister. Recruits began pulling out their masks and the instructor pulled them from their hands and yelled, "I have not given the order to deploy masks!" The gas engulfed the chamber as panicking recruits forgot they had masks and started screaming thinking they were being gassed. Those close to the wooden walls began trying to scrape their way out. Many had fingernails that were bent backwards with blood streaming down their arms. I was toward the middle of the room, and fortunately, did not panic. My eyes were filled and flowing with tears. The skin on my face and arms was burning. Fluid was flowing profusely from my nose. It was a very uncomfortable experience. I noticed, however, the symptoms stabilized after a few minutes. Just then, the door was opened and everyone rushed out.

The instructor told us the second exercise was to show us the effects of the gas without a mask. If we were in a situation without a mask we could manage to stay in control. I got that, but I'm not sure others did. The instructor told us that anyone who could smoke a whole cigarette in the chamber without a mask would have full smoking privileges the rest of training. Guess who volunteered? I lit up and along with another guy entered the chamber. The instructor came in, dropped a canister, left, and locked the door. I knew if I cuffed the cigarette with my hand I could keep the cigarette dry as I smoked it. The other guy did not think of this and his cigarette soon got wet and burned out. The instructor opened the door a few minutes later and found that my cigarette was smoked down and still burning. He told the other guy to go sit down and made me an example of an accomplishment under the effects of tear gas.

My DI told me to come with him around the side of the building, away from those seated in the bleachers. Once around the corner he told me:

"You are a XXXX, XXXX, XXXXing idiot to smoke a XXXXing cigarette in the XXXXing gas chamber and you would never get XXXXing special smoking privileges."

While a monument to stupidity, I still think it was quite a feat. This incident was avenged on a day, thirty-five years ago, when my first son was born. On that day, I quit smoking cold turkey and have not smoked since.

Lady of Chinju

Based on a true story of honor.

WHILE WORKING IN FORT WORTH, TEXAS, ON AN ENGI-neering contract assigned to an aircraft company, I was sent to Chinju, also spelled Jinju, South Korea. Ordinarily, company direct employees sop up any overseas opportunities, but Chinju is no Paris or Düsseldorf. Let's face it, how many travel brochures have you seen for South Korea? Chinju is located in the southern end of the country far from Seoul or any other metro center where there are at least some western influences. Only two people at the hotel spoke some basic English. One of them gave me a Korean phrase to keep in my wallet to give to someone if I got lost. It said: *Take me to the Dong Bang Hotel.*

I did manage to visit the Chinju Fortress several times. This large very peaceful facility, built in approximately 1379 of huge cut and fit boulders, has withstood the test of time. During the constant incursions by the Japanese, the huge fortress bell was rung and the local villagers would rush into the fortress. The women would dress as soldiers and deploy on the hill within the fortress to make the trained fighting force look larger than it was. The villagers, alongside the local military forces, would fend off the attacks. Throughout Korean history the fortress changed hands many times between various forces.

Today, inside the fortress there are several large pagodas. One of these beautiful ornate pagodas was dedicated to a Korean woman, Nongae, for her dedication during a Japanese occupation.

"General Agumy, are you comfortable?"

"Why, yes, Nongae, thank you. You are always very considerate, not like the typical Korean women attendants. They seem to hate us. We protect them and allow them to have a life and the privilege to pay money to the Japanese government. Nongae, stay in attendance."

The General motions to a guard and says: "Summon my staff."

A short time later during a staff meeting:
"I am not happy with the respect we are getting from the Korean community. They should bow to us for what we are giving them. We are Gods and they are lowly dirt. They are defeated and should start acting like it. From now on any citizen who does not snap to attention in our presence, especially mine, will be beaten. Make sure others see the beatings. Be sure though, that after a day's beating, they are still able to labor the following day. The Japanese government counts on their backs bent over and working."

"Now, get out of here and start beating people."

The General glances over at Nongae. She sits quietly with her head bowed.

"Lieutenant Lu, I would like this Korean girl, Nongae, to be in my daily attendance. I want her available at all times ... especially at night."

Over the following months the General enforces even harsher civil directives over the enslaved Korean people. He encourages the growth of Korean families. He envisions

28

thousands of Korean children, like locust, swarming in fields harvesting crops for the glory of Japan.

He and Nongae spend more time together than any of the other female attendants. He begins to confide in her and occasionally seeks her council on matters relating to the Korean people. One day he asks her:

"Nongae, what are you trained to do."

"I was studying acting. When your forces came into Chinju they burned down our theatre company."

"I will see to it that your people rebuild it. We will teach your people what real theatre productions are and charge them dearly to attend each play. Your people owe us dearly for the gift of life. We could have slaughtered them all.

"Thank you, General. You are so generous. General, if you please I would like be involved with the rebuilding of the new theatre. I feel I could motivate my people to work on this project. It will provide entertainment for you and your soldiers."

"Yes, Nongae, I will see that you have the materials and guards to push the builders. I see it as a real money maker."

Soon afterward, on a rainy May day, the new theatre was completed.

The General and Nongae would often take afternoon walks together. One day, Nongae asked the General to go for a swim, instead of a walk. The river was adjacent to the fortress. He consented.

While out in the middle of the river, they laughed and splashed in the cool water. Nongae worked her way behind him and wrapped her arms and legs tightly around him. As he struggled helplessly to stay above the surface, Nongae whispered in his ear:

"This performance is for you, General."

After a short struggle their lifeless bodies began to separate and float down the river. The General's guards tried in vain to revive the General. Nongae's body continued down the river, into the open arms of National respect and honor.

Each year, in May, the Nongae Festival is celebrated including a reenactment of the courageous suicidal drowning.

Culinary Adventures with Norman

There is only one Norman. God love him.

NORMAN SATANOSKI AND I HAVE BEEN FRIENDS FOR MANY years. I love him like a brother and we have had many laughs over the years. Here are some of our adventures together.

Adventure #1: Try not to laugh too hard.
When I was in my early thirties my friends and I rented a cottage every summer on Cape Cod. We seldom ate out but one night about twelve of us decided to go out to dinner together. I was seated next to my buddy, the one-and-only Norman. The table was buzzing with the days talk and people were looking and commenting on the menu. I recall Norman saying something like he was not very hungry. The waitress came by and one-by-one took our order. Shortly thereafter, she and an assistant reappeared to serve the orders. She placed Norman's order in front of him. It looked like a plate of hors d' oeuvres.

"Excuse me, excuse me, miss." Norman said. "I believe I got the wrong order."

"What did you order, sir?" the waitress asked. With that, all conversation around the table stopped.

Norman said:

"I ordered hors-de-ovaries."

Adventure #2: Oh no ...

One summer on the Cape, Norman and I decided to dig up clams in the mucky backwater and have a clam dinner. We went down to the local Town Hall and bought a one-day license to dig clams. They gave us a clam ring and told us that any clams that passed through the ring had to be thrown back. Soon, we were calf deep in the bay with our clam rakes hard at work. It didn't take long for us to get the hang of it. Within several hours we had a pail full of legal size Cherrystone Clams.

We decided to shuck the clams, roll them in breading, and deep-fry them to make fried clams. It took us two hours to prepare the clams for the pot. I put oil in a pot and put it on the stove. Soon, there was steam coming up from the pot.

"Are we ready to go, Norman?"

"Yeh, we look good. The oil looks hot enough. Let's dump them in."

In the clams went. The pot contents immediately exploded and boiled over with this horrible sizzling sound. We had boiling oil all over the stove, floor, and wall. What a mess! Our clams were burnt offerings, blackened, and shriveled down the size of a pea. It took two hours to clean up the oil that had spilled all over the kitchen. Then, reluctantly, we headed out for dinner.

Adventure #3: *The Unhappy Fireman*

Norman and I shared a terrific apartment in Boston. The apartment was on the fifth floor but back then we didn't mind the walk up. Our living room windows overlooked St. Botolph Street. The apartment below us had a large Bay window that extended out right below our middle window. The slightly sloping roof of the Bay window was right below our window ledge and flat enough for Norman's hibachi grill.

One night, we had steaks ablaze on the grill. Both of us were leaning out the window, checking our steaks, when we heard screaming sirens. Sirens are no stranger to the streets of Boston, but these sirens were attached to a huge fire truck that slammed its brakes on right in front of our building. We looked above us and then over to the adjacent buildings but there was no fire. On the street below, firemen were scurrying around in concert. Soon the telescoping ladder rotated over in our direction and a fireman with a hose was headed up towards us. Before we knew it he was at eye level. He looked at our flaming steaks on the grill, and said:

"You guys got to be shit'n me."

Evidently, someone saw flames shooting up from the top of the Bay window and called the fire station.

Adventure 4: *Norman!!!!!!!*

Our summers on the Cape were one party after another. Either, our friends from "Snug Harbor" had one or the "A" Framers, my group, did. Our "A" Frame parties got to be so big that we had committees to make sure that everything went off well. I was usually on the parking committee with three fairly sober buddies on my staff. One party, Norman was sole Chairman responsible for the purchase of corn on the cob.

We had determined that for this particular weekend blast we needed four bushels of corn. Norman said he'd take care of it. Now ... how does four bushels of corn turn into sixteen bushels? Easily, if Norman has anything to do with it. Norman was going to get the four bushels, but decided to ask Tommy Ruby who lived closer to a local farm. A few days later, he heard Tommy was sick so he asked Marty "Millions" DeMatteo to pick it up. Later that day, he realized that a busy guy like Marty would not be able to get the corn so he asked Billy Batty. Then on Friday, the day before the party, Norman, thinking everyone would forget, bought four bushels of corn. Well, as you may have guessed, everyone who Norman asked brought corn. That's how four bushels of corn turns into sixteen bushels! Norman!!!!!

It Was The Best Time!

Lots of gin & tonic and lots of laughs.

I TALKED WITH MY BUDDY, NORMAN, RECENTLY ABOUT THIS *story and he told me:*

"When you have owned a wooden sailboat you tend to forget the past. My boat was 25'-6" long, that's 306 inches. I've sanded every inch of it, many times. I sold it thirty-five years ago and I still have undercoating in my hair."

As we talked, however, the memories of his first sea voyage with his new boat came back. Along with a big smile, I might add.

In the spring of 1974, Norman had just returned to Boston from the ski season in Vermont. He found a sailboat and bought it for $600. He named her *Sugarbush*. She was a beauty and Norman was frothing at the bit to take his first trip with her.

That summer, when a bunch of us were sharing a cottage on Cape Cod, Norman announced a Gin & Tonic Cruise to Martha's Vineyard. He only had two takers: myself, and 'Iron Mike' Ruby.

When Mike and I showed up at 9a.m. for the trip, there was no gin or tonic … textbook Norman. 'Iron Mike' and

I went to the store and made sure the hold was bulging with gin, tonic, limes, and ice, enough to choke a horse.

Shortly after, the sails filled and we set out of Woods Hole. Soon, it was apparent that we had a tough row to hoe. Since the prevailing winds were in our face, we were looking at tacking the sailboat for the nine miles to Oak Bluffs Harbor, on Martha Vineyard.

"Well, surf's up. Cocktails, gentlemen? " I asked.

Within minutes the cocktails were being sipped in the salty breezes. We decided that each right tack was at least worth one cocktail. The sails were full and so were we ... with gin and tonic. Nine right tacks later, and five hours later, we were entering the inlet of the harbor. We dropped sail and continued under motor power.

The harbor entrance was narrow. As we lined up within the channel, a tugboat was approaching us leaving the harbor. To our amazement, the tugboat was towing a huge Great White Shark. We rubbed our bloodshot eyes, but there was no doubt what we had seen. We reasoned that the shark had entered the small harbor and the authorities used a stun gun to subdue the beast and were dragging it out to sea.

We continued into the harbor. The wind had shifted and we realized that we would have to tack back to Woods Hole. Norman assessed his crew's fitness for duty and decided we were not fit to walk let alone work a sailboat. We decided to split a slip and put in for the night.

Our assigned slip was between two very large yachts. The *Invincible* registered in Bermuda was to the left of our slip and the *Pride* of Newport News, on the right. Both ships had several levels of decks. As we approached our slip, we got the attention of party goers on the *Invincible*. This was Norman's first time bringing his boat into a slip.

"Norman, Norman, cut our speed, cut, cut!" I yelled.

"We're going way too fast Norman! Way too fast!" screamed 'Iron Mike.'

We were running at ramming speed at high tide, and then, *BANG* ... we slammed into the dock. We were thrown forward, but somehow the crew and *Sugarbush* had survived.

We secured the boat and went into town for dinner and a night of fun and frivolity. Since we already had plenty of wind in our sails, we fell easily into a night of partying. We found out that the shark we saw was a movie prop for a movie being filmed called *Jaws*. I remember saying to the guys,

"Who's going to pay money to see another stupid shark movie?"

Late into the evening we wandered into a local bar near the harbor. There was no one in the place except us. We sat at the bar and waited to be served. When no one appeared, I became our bartender:

"Well ... surf's up. Cocktails, gentlemen? " I asked.

We sat there for some two hours, helping ourselves. We placed a pile of money on the bar and left. Soon, singing and bouncing off each other, we made it back to the boat.

One problem:

When we secured the boat at high tide we just stepped off the front deck and onto the dock. Now, at low tide, the boat deck was much lower than the level of the dock. The only way to get on the boat was to jump and the deck was covered with morning dew.

Norman went first. As soon as it hit the deck, his shoes slipped on the dew and he was in the drink. Norman pulled himself up into the boat. Mike and I laughed to tears. Mike went next and suffered the same fate. It should be of no surprise that I was soon soaked too. We all crawled underneath the front deck, packed like sardines, and crashed.

We woke up the next morning a ball of sweat because the mid-morning sun was pounding on the front deck. We were still wet and smelled awful.

'Iron Mike' said, "I'm totally rusted. I can't move."

Norman just sat there holding his head and moaning. My eyes were burning. My wet clothes were stuck to me. My head was pounding to the beat of *The Battle Hymn of the Republic*: a pounding that could set a building piling.

It Was The Best Time!

Test Procedure Step 97

A motive, a killer, a robot, and a computer.

ACTON ROBOTICS IS A SUPERSTAR IN THE FIELD OF ROBOT-ics. The founder, Harold Acton, has guided the company from its inception to a market leader with a best of breed stock. One reason for the company's success is it's dedication to specialty robots: robots tailored to specific client applications. While their client base is limited, there is plenty of demand for specialty robotic applications.

Mr. Acton was invited to an international convention on Robotics to accept an award for his contributions to the industry:

"Ladies and gentlemen. There can be no doubt that robotics will continue to be a major player in manufacturing and will soon be a part of every day life. I thank you for this award. It represents all the hard work I have put into my passion for robotics. Thank you."

Recently a large museum had requested the company to develop a surveillance robot. The robot must be capable of silently performing visual, motion, and sound surveillance throughout the museum without disturbing the existing similar surveillance systems. While the development of such a robot is a challenge, Action Robotics was up to the task.

Harold French, Chief Design Engineer, and a long-time employee, has begun the conceptual design. Within a month, his staff of engineers had come up with a stealthy design. Max Wetzel, software engineer, began developing the software for the project.

"Max," said Harold:

"I'm sick and tired of that old SOB getting all the credit for our robots. I'm not going to work any more weekends just so he can take all the credit for an early shipment. I have been granted twenty-three patents and never got any credit for them."

"How about how cheap he is, too," said Max.

"That bastard hasn't given me a raise in three years. When I confronted him last month he laughed and said I was lucky I had a job."

Just then Mr. Acton appeared.

"So ... Harold. Is the prototype for the Collins Museum about ready for testing? Say ... why does this robot have the full hand rotation and function package? I don't believe their specification called for this feature. After all, this robot is for surveillance."

"Yes, Mr. Acton, it's in the Lab. Max is working on final software tweaks. Jimmy is working on approval of the testing procedure. I need to get it back up to the Shop. They installed the advanced hand function feature by mistake. I'll take care of it."

"OK ... Let's keep this well ahead of schedule. We need to be sure that this thing is silent during testing. The museum has very sensitive sound surveillance."

A week later, Mr. Acton and the design staff is in the lab putting the robot through its paces. It's toward the end of the day and only Max and Mr. Acton remain in the lab.

Max is rummaging through draws to look for a piece of equipment and comes upon the gun that they keep in the lab. He checks the chamber and finds it loaded.

"Mr. Acton, when was the last time you had this gun cleaned?"

"Well … It's been awhile. I need to get to that. Why are you wearing gloves, Max?"

"I hate guns, I don't even like touching them. I'll leave it out so you remember to get it cleaned."

"OK. Hey … Let's try something. Move the robot over behind me and move it around. I'm going to listen and see if I can hear it."

"Yeh … That's an interesting test. Instead of doing it right now, I've got a few things to do. I'll do it when you are not expecting it."

Max goes about his business and at 6p.m. says:

"OK … Goodnight, Mr. Acton."

"Wait … How about the test?"

"I already did it about twenty minutes ago and you never even budged."

"Wow … That's what I call a successful test, Max. Good night."

That night, Max and Harold went bowling together. The next morning there was a lot of commotion at the office. The cleaning crew reported that about 8p.m. they found Mr. Acton slumped in his lab chair with a pool of blood beneath him. His arms were hanging lifeless at his side. At the base of his right arm was a gun.

Max casually walked over to his desk and turned on his computer. After logging on, he brought up the test procedure, highlighted Step 97 and hit Delete.

Later that day, Max ran into Harold in the break room. Quietly Max said:

"Well, Harold … we certainly put the "S" in Specialty!"

41

Tales from West Island

Some fun stories about my college days with Pete.

BACK WHEN I WAS IN COLLEGE, MY ROOMMATE, PETE DONnelly and I shared a small cottage on West Island. It is a small island off the Massachusetts coast, near New Bedford. During the winter, back in the early '70's, the island was desolate. Pete was Oceanography major, and I was a Mechanical Engineering major.

One of my fondest memories was accompanying Pete on his walks through the estuaries and inter-tidal zones that surrounded the island. He was drawn there and so was I. These waters were often teeming with sea anemone, crabs, sea cucumbers, sea urchins, and hundreds, perhaps thousands, of forms of sea life. We wandered for hours looking at all of God's creatures living lives so different than ours. The water was crystal clear and on a sunny day the inter-tidal zones exploded with color and sea life. Pete would always talk about the complex marine ecosystem. It was so interesting to me how temperature, salinity, and Ph balance, along with other factors, were important to maintain a healthy ecosystem.

While Pete and I had little or no time to ourselves, our retired neighbor, Mr. Steed, had plenty, maybe too much, time to himself. He spent most of his day shining up his garden tractor and fussing over his grass. If a small dead branch fell on the lawn, a branch that he could easily just walk out to and pickup, he would spring into action. His back door would fly open and he would rush over and open the garage door, hop on his tractor, back up, drive over to where his utility wagon was stored, back up and attach his utility wagon. He would drive out onto the lawn adjacent to the small branch, load it into his wagon, and take it over to his debris pile. Then, he would drive back, back up and park the utility wagon, then drive his tractor back into the garage. After he closed the garage door he would stand and admire his lawn, then turn, returning to the house. It was just another busy day for Mr. Steed.

One day when a friend was over we told him about Mr. Steed. He found it hard to believe. As it happened, Mr. Steed was not home at the time. I ran out and put a small stick on his lawn before he got home. Sure enough, before he brought his groceries into the house, he spotted the stick, and fired up his tractor. This was fun to watch but it didn't pay the bills.

We both had part time jobs while attending classes, but we were always just scraping by financially. Our favorite cheap eat was Garlacko Spaghetti. Ahhhh ... yes, lots of fresh sliced garlic. Here's the recipe:

GARLACKO SPAGHETTI

Lots of fresh sliced garlic. Slice until your arm is tired.

2 T Olive Oil

4 T Butter (no substitutions)

1 lb Spaghetti

Parmesan Cheese (if desired)

Sauté the garlic slices to a golden brown in olive oil. Add four big tablespoons of butter. Simmer. Boil one pound of spaghetti (do not overcook). Thoroughly drain the spaghetti and mix with the garlic sauce. Serve with crusty bread layered with lots of butter. Leave the butter dish out one hour before dinner. Serves two hungry guys. Keep your distance from anyone for about three days!

The Christmas of our senior year, our neighbor across the street brought home this giant Christmas tree and managed to force it through his front door. I knew the tree could not possibly fit in his small house, so I was not surprised when he cut off the bottom two feet of the tree and dragged it out to the curb.

I dragged it into our place and we had ourselves a Christmas tree. It was only two feet tall and about ten feet in diameter, but looked great after we added lights and homemade ornaments mainly to the top of the tree. In the middle of tree, on the top, Pete placed an Angel. Pete said the Angel looked like his love interest Joan.

Pete had been trying to get a date with a lady from school named Joan. As much as he tried, he couldn't get to first base with her. She drove an old car and constantly had problems with it. Back in those days anyone could lift your engine hood. Anytime Joan had car trouble she would call Pete. He made many trips all over town working on her car. Most of the time it was some sort of electrical problem. Numerous times Joan would say to Pete:

"Thanks so much for fixing my car. I want to have you over for a duck dinner some time. I cook a great duck."

One day, in early January, Joan called and said the battery Pete had given her and installed was dead. Pete had given her the battery months before and told her it was an old battery and that she should buy a new one. Of course, she didn't. She had promised him a duck dinner at Christmas for all the work he had done on her car. Of course, that didn't happen either.

On that frigid January day, Pete asked me to come along to fix her car. He said to me:

"Don, I'm fixing Joan's car for the last time. You'll want to be there for this."

We located her car and opened the hood. Pete disconnected the battery terminals and removed his old battery. He asked me to bring him the bag that was in his trunk. I returned with the bag. He opened the bag and took out a duck that he had purchased at an Asian market. He put the duck in the battery tray and connected a battery lead to each leg of the duck. He closed the hood and we laughed all the way home. That was the last of Joan.

Thank You ...

You never know who will come to your aid when the chips are down.

FOLKS IN SLEEPY GUEYDAN, VERMILION PARISH, LOUISIANA, *still tell this story today, even though it took place so long ago. The story about a little boy and a big alligator. One hot, sweaty, August afternoon in 1904, innocence and beast would meet.*

Gueydan, even today, does not get many visitors. The sleepy, out of the way town and adjacent marshes suits many of its residents ... and it's alligators just fine. In Gueydan, the Marceaux family goes way back. In 1895, Beau Marceaux met Clara Willis at a church dance when Beau was working on the rail extension for the Louisiana Western Railroad. Shortly after that, they were married and soon Tagi Maye was born. Two years later, little Willy B. was born.

They lived on Daspit Street, not far from Main Street. Beau continued to work for the railroad and Clara did what she loved, homemaking. Life was quiet in Gueydan, but good. Sure, there were hurricanes, hot spells and such, but Clara would look out from her porch everyday and thank God for what she and her family had.

Every Sunday after church, Clara and Tagi Maye would spend precious time together in the kitchen. Clara enjoyed teaching Tagi Maye cooking, sewing, and general homemaking skills. Tagi Maye loved this time together. Some lucky guy someday would be enjoying a slice of Tagi Maye's strawberry-rhubarb pie.

Most Sundays, Beau and little Willy would rush off south in the buckboard, down seven some odd miles of dusty, bumpy, dirt roads headed for the swamps. Their fishing poles, tackle boxes, and lunch were lashed down so they could not fly out.

Willy and his dad loved fishing the swamp together. They had a small row boat hidden in the reeds that gave them access to the catfish, crappie, and large mouth bass that thrived in the muddy water. The swamp was chocked full of wildlife including snakes, birds, and various reptiles, including alligators.

Willy loved nature and his dad encouraged him. Willy was fascinated with alligators. Occasionally, they would catch one by accident. Beau would struggle to get the hook out of the gators tough jaws. Most of the time Beau had to just cut the line. He had no use for alligators.

Willy had names for all the alligators he often saw where they would fish. His favorite though was Old Lumpie. Old Lumpie had several scars on his snout and a big brown and black multi faceted lump under his right eye. He was a big gator, at least ten feet. When Old Lumpie came near the old boat, and he did often, Willy would call out to him and throw out handfuls of minnows. The water would turn black as the gator swirled to grab all the fish. Willy had seen the gators in action plenty of times and his dad often cautioned him about the dangers. "Take shed of feedin' dem gators," Beau would often say. "Day scare dem cats away." Willy often wondered how Old Lumpie got that big lump under his eye.

Sometimes Tagi Maye went fishing but would usually rather spend the day with her mom. On a good day there would be catfish a plenty. Clara showed Tagi Maye how to make her spicy cornmeal breading. Clara would say a blessing and dinner was often an elbow flying event, and quick as Spring, empty plates. Tagi Maye would remove the plates and Willy would always forget to say, "thank you." Tagi Maye would always say "Willy ... Did you forgit somethan?"

"Paw Paw ... Why do you expect old Lumpie always looks the same?" asked Willy. "He never smiles."

"Well, I expect he's got nothing to be a smilin' for."

"He seems pretty happy when I throw him some fish. He never says, "thank you." I guess gators never say, "thank you." Tagi Maye always makes sure I say, "thank you."

On one Sunday, Willy and Beau pushed the boat out of the reeds and paddled over to their favorite spot. Willy had some big night crawlers that he grabbed after last nights rain. Within minutes, lines were in the water and anticipation was in the air.

"Sure is a nice day Willy. Good things happen on nice days I expect."

After a spell ... *Wham!* Something big hit Willy's pole. "Willy, hold on" said Beau. Willy had never seen his pole bend such. Beau jumped up to grab the net. He stepped forward, but caught his foot on the seat and fell, hitting his head. Beau was not moving. Willy began to realize that his dad was knocked out. Willy began to panic. He tried to get Paw Paw to move, then stood up to push him to the middle of the boat. His dad had always told him to keep weight in the boat toward the center. Willy stood up to yell for help but lost his balance, falling over the gunnel and into the murky water. Willy could not swim. He flailed helplessly, screaming for his dad, to no avail. He struggled to keep his head above water but soon disappeared in the muddy water. His last vision was the boat moving away with the wind.

Suddenly, Willy felt himself being lifted up above the water surface. He found himself on Lumpie's snout moving rapidly toward shore. Willy hung onto Lumpie for dear life. Lumpie slid up the bank and Willy rolled off. Lumpie tipped his snout and slid backwards back into the murky water. Willy was exhausted and lay silently on the bank.

Beau slowly regained consciousness and sat up. He was feverishly looking for Willy and cried out. Willy called back from the muddy bank.

"Thank you, Father!" cried out Beau. "Willy, what you be doin' on de bank?"

"I fell outta de boat, and Old Lumpie fetched me."

Back home on Daspit Street, Willy, along with his dad, recounted the story to his mother and Tagi Maye. All sat quietly in amazement listening to the whopper of a fishing story.

"Hallelujah! Good things happen on nice days!" said Beau.

Willy turned to Tagi Maye:

"Oh, Tagi Maye ... when Old Lumpie plopped me down on de bank, I said, "Thank you.""

The Hill

Some fun stories about days on Beacon Hill in Boston.

WHEN I FIRST SAW BEACON HILL IN BOSTON I KNEW I had to live there. The narrow tree lined streets, some of them cobblestone, rising to a vanishing point at the top of the hill. The hustle and bustle. It was all intoxicating. It was the late '60s and political disobedience and partying were in the air.

Mister Sleepy:
I shared my first apartment, a fifth floor walkup, with my buddy, Kenny McAuley. We both were attending Northeast Institute of Industrial Technology, otherwise known as good old NIT. It was Beacon Hill's only institution of higher learning. When asked where I went to college, I would say,

"Oh, I go to NIT."

"Wow … MIT. Great school'"

I soon stopped disappointing people when I told them NIT, not MIT. So, I just said:

"Why yes … it is."

Kenny and I, ever the rule breakers, were renting an apartment, against school policy. Students were limited to either live at home or in the one school dormitory. Our apartment was a five-minute walk to our campus, which consisted of a three-story building on the corner of two streets. As far as the school knew, I lived at home, in Framingham, about thirty miles west of Boston.

I was not very good at getting up early for school, especially on Mondays. It could have something to do with the fact that we partied from 5p.m. on Friday straight through to 11p.m. on Sunday. It took all of the following week to catch up. So, it was just a matter of time before my stumbling in late to class caught up with me.

"Mr. Lee, it has come to my attention that you have been tardy twenty-seven times this quarter. That's 14.2 times the student average. Now, we have students that come in from way out, like New Hampshire and Vermont. You only have to come from Framingham, thirty miles away. What do you have to say for yourself?"

It took every muscle in my body to control myself from bursting out laughing. If he only knew I lived five-minutes away!

"Mr. Tarbox, I want you to know that I value my education above all else in my life right now. I assure you in all my academic endeavors I will commit to 100% of the absolute minimum attendance. I have undergone a self-evaluation and have decided to allow myself more time to get to school in the morning. You will see an improvement. My goal is to improve my tardiness to only 5.3 times the student average."

Just Getting By:
Following graduation, I shared an apartment with Kenny on the second floor of the building located at West Cedar

Street on the Hill. Kenny and I found work with an electronics company in Cambridge. Neither of us had any real money back then. The cost of rent and utilities seriously cut into our social budget.

We soon discovered if you fell behind with your utility bills, the companies would give you three months to pay up. If you didn't pay up, the power, water, gas, or whatever was shut off. So, three months before our lease ended, we asked our buddy, Louie Talent, to move in and put all the accounts in his name.

Louie Talent is well known by the city of Boston utility companies. If anyone ever asks you about him, you never met him. Distance is your ally when it comes to Louie. He received many, perhaps hundreds, of angry phone calls from the various utility companies. Not one of the calls was ever returned.

Johnnie Mulvihill (#3), a buddy of ours, enjoyed taking the calls and messages for Louie:

"Hello. This Marilyn Reeves calling from Boston Gas. I really must speak with Mr. Talent."

"Might I ask what the subject of this call pertains to?" asked Johnnie.

"I really must talk to Mr. Talent. Is he there?"

"Oh ... I'm so sorry, you just missed him, maybe two minutes ago. He went to his yacht piloting class in the harbor. May I take a message?"

I'm sure Louie still has the worst credit rating in the city of Boston. Of course, as you may guess, Louie never existed. At times, maybe that's the best kind of roommate.

It wasn't just us that struggled getting by back then. There were two ladies that lived across the street from us who went to the New England School of Embalming. Instead of beds, they slept in caskets that they had borrowed from school. Yes, they were a little creepy. All of us were always looking for ways to save money.

Back then, you could put a bogus address on an envelope with no stamp and use the person's address you wanted the mail to go to as the return address. Then, when the Post Office saw no stamp, they would return the mail to the return address. We also cut out things that looked like a stamp, cut it to size, and glued it on an envelope. Post Office fraud was not our only form of entertainment.

Urban Entertainment:
We always had parties, mainly with the student nurses from Massachusetts General Hospital. We drank gallons of Vin Rose wine because a half-gallon jug was $1.75. All of my buddy's were such characters. After a party ended, an inebriated Paul Zmuda would sneak into the subway tunnel just east of the Charles Street Station, at the end of Lindall Street. He loved to walk the subway tunnels after the system closed down at night. One night, he went into the tunnel with a big burlap sack and returned with a load of high wattage bulbs ... you know, the ones that are coated with this yellowish, brown film. Claude Soones would take us anywhere we wanted to go with philosophy. Norman spun his Beatles albums and Dave Zywno entertained all with his Ditty-Bop dancing. Dave often reminded us that his name was always the last name in any phone book.

Our living room faced West Cedar Street. My love of fishing led me to be creative. I invented urban wallet fishing. I had an old wallet that I fastened to the end of my spinning line. After dark, I'd lean out the window and cast the wallet down the sidewalk running along the building. It took skill to land the wallet without snagging a tree limb. It would not be long until someone would walk up, notice the wallet, stop, look around in all directions, and then stoop down to pick-up the wallet. Sometimes I'd yank it right out of their hands, other times I'd wait until they opened it. Sometimes, I'd wait until they reached down, then, reel it in a few inches. One day, this guy chased the wallet about twenty feet! Rain or shine, I always caught something.

Opening Day:
One night over lots of vino we all decided to go fishing on opening day of trout season. We chose Lake Cochituate, located about twenty-five miles west of Boston, in Natick. The season started a 6a.m. that April day and we planned to get there early to get a good spot. Realistically, getting up around 3a.m. to dress, pack our gear, and drive out to the lake was not an option, so we decided to go straight out from our wine fest.

There was me, Kenny, Paul, Joe Grassa, Norman Satanoski, and Dicky Mauldin. We changed our clothes, grabbed our gear, and were on the road by 3a.m. We got to Natick about 4a.m. and found an open all night Dunkin' Donut shop. We stuffed down donuts and coffee down and felt semi-okay.

Then, we promptly got lost but managed to get to the lake about 5a.m. It was still pitch dark and we were not feeling all that well. We parked and started walking around the shoreline looking for a good spot. Paul, walking very close to the water's edge, slipped on some slick mud and fell in sideways. Dicky rushed over to help Paul, but both his legs slipped from under him and he was in the drink too. As they floundered to get out, slipping on the mud, we all had a good laugh. We checked our gear and got our lines ready. Within a few minutes hundreds of fisherman lined the shore. At the stroke of 6a.m. about

400 pounds of metal lures hit the waters surface. I thought there was going to be a Tsunami!

Kenny decided to cast out under an overhanging tree. His cast was on target until his line got tangled in the lowest branch. He began whipping his rod around to try to free the lure with no luck. Against Joe's advice, he climbed the tree and was shimmying out on a long branch to reach the lure. The lure was one foot from his grasp when the branch snapped and he ended up soaking wet also. Of course, Joe laughed the hardest. I remember laughing so hard that I almost fell in. We fished another hour or so, telling old stories. That's why fishing is so rewarding. It's not important to catch fish, just to relax and enjoy each other's company.

Just before we left, when I was not paying attention, they pushed me in and as tired as we were, we all laughed. I have always loved fishing.

Now on the downhill side of life, my love for fishing has led me to be a fisher-of-men. We all are asked to do this. I have answered the call and now cast in all directions. I find it truly satisfying.

Collections, Anyone?:

One Saturday morning we were sitting around and #3 was skimming the paper for jobs. He needed one more job search contact for his weekly unemployment. He noticed an ad posted by a collection agency. The ad read:

Collection Associate sought for aggressive growing business. Must be persuasive, relentless, imposing, and will not accept "no" for an answer. Please call 617-567-0990, ask for Rocco.

#3 decided to call:

"Yeh ... Rocco."

"Yes, Mr. Rocco, this is Johnnie Mulvihill. I am interested in the advertisement you have in the paper for a Collection Associate."

"Yeh, well, for starters, my first name is Rocco. No last names. We are looking for someone who we can send out and they come back with the money, no matter what it takes to do it. What experience do you have in collections?

"Well, I was the lead alter boy at Saint Bartholomew's for past three years."

I can still hear the bang of the phone being slammed down by Rocco.

Mission Impossible:

We used to go down the Charles Street Steak House every Sunday, late afternoon. A T-bone steak was $1.75. We would always complain because a baked potato was 10 cents extra. After our steak dinner we would rush home and watch *Mission Impossible*.

Myself, Johnnie Mulvihill (#3) and Joe Fravel lived together at that time. Joe worked at the shipyards in Quincy and would always come home after work exhausted. He would put a TV dinner in the oven then fall asleep on the couch. Many times he would wake up to a burnt dinner. One day we decided to pull a 'Mission Impossible' on Joe. The plan was to wait until his dinner was done, shut off the oven, and recreate the typical morning scene so he would think he slept through the night on the couch. Since it was fall, it was just as dark at 8p.m. as it was at 5a.m. We set back all the clocks to 5a.m. and dressed in our pj's and woke him up:

"Joe … Joe … get up, it's 5a.m."

"It is? Gosh, I hardly feel as if I've got any sleep."

Joe waited until I got out of the shower, just like every morning, brushed his teeth, dressed, and went out the door. Three minutes later he came back through the door:
"You bastards!"
We chanted: "Dun, Dun, Dun, Dah, Dah, Dah.

Fresh Air:
After work, weather permitting, you would find Johnnie and I out on West Cedar Street throwing the Frisbee to each other. It's amazing what control you can develop with practice. Both Johnnie and I were (and still are) incurable leg men. As the ladies who lived in the neighborhood were walking home after work, we often rated their legs: "I'll give that one a solid eight." The coveted ten was never rendered.

There were lots of interesting characters that passed by also: A buddy of ours, 'T-bone,' was always dressed up as a biker and had a falcon tethered to the appellate on his black leather jacket. He drove an old beat up scooter because he couldn't afford a real bike. There was a lady who sold newspapers yelling out "BAD" {Boston After Dark) riding on the rims of a bicycle that had no rubber tires. Our favorite though, was a disgusted look we always got from one young lady no matter how politely we said, "hello."

Meeting the 'Turk':
As related to me, one night Johnnie and my other buddy 'Iron Mike' Ruby, went down to the Harvard Gardens, on Cambridge Street, for a few brewskies. They sat down at the crowded bar. As they were throwing them down, Johnnie went to the men's room. 'Iron Mike' turned to his wide-eyed neighbor. 'Iron Mike' could sense his zest for life:

"Excuse me, sir. Did you notice who I'm sitting next to?" said 'Iron Mike.'

"No, I'm sorry, I didn't."

"It's Derek Sanderson," said 'Iron Mike.'

"Wow ... Derek 'Turk' Sanderson, the retired Bruins defenseman?"

Derek Sanderson was a standout defenseman for the Boston Bruins from 1968 through 1972. He was a member of the 1970 and 1972 winning Stanley Cup hockey teams. He won numerous awards, and was known as a tough guy on the ice, and for a flamboyant lifestyle that endeared him to the public. Johnnie looked a lot like Derek, especially after a few drinks.

Before Johnnie got a chance to sit down the man said:

"Sir, this is such an honor to meet you. It wasn't covered much in the press, but I remember in the 69-70 Stanley Cup, game four, only forty seconds into overtime, you centered the winning goal to Bobby Orr. Could I have your autograph?"

"I told you he was Derek, didn't I," said 'Iron Mike.'

Johnnie just decided to play along.

"Sure, I'll sign. Wow, you have some memory. Thanks for relating that story." Johnnie said.

Soon the word got around the bar and Mike and Johnnie were surrounded by a crowd of well-wishers, buying drinks and rehashing old hockey tales. One guy asked Johnnie if he would call his son from a phone booth to say,"hello." Johnnie, of course, complied.

The White Lie:
Sometimes it's OK to tell a white lie:

White Lie: A lie that does not hurt anyone, usually well intended, and can be justified by the end result. I don't think you will find this definition anywhere because I made it up.

If you came upon a friend of ours, Steve Tersiak, in an alley it would be unnerving. He was average height and weight, but his eyes were constantly shifting. His eyes moved from side to side, up and down, and often seemed to move independently, one looking up, and the other looking to the side. When you spoke with him you were never sure which eye to look into. His wild man look made it difficult to meet the ladies.

Steve was a parking attendant at a local parking garage in a condominium adjacent to Massachusetts General Hospital. We liked Steve. Despite his wild man look he always smiled and was friendly. Many of the student nurses from the hospital stayed in this condominium. The nurses always came to our parties and we were always chasing them around.

One day, after we had piled out of one of the nurse's cars, Steve called us over:

"How do you guys do it? Every time I see you guys, you have beautiful women draped all over you and having a blast. I don't have a girlfriend. Even when I get a woman somewhat interested, as soon as I tell them I'm a parking attendant, they walk off."

We decided to ask Steve to our parties in hopes he would meet someone. Well, our buddy Steve didn't do all that well. One night, after many beverages, one of us came up with a brilliant idea:

Steve needed an identity, a nickname, something to make him interesting. From then on, he was known as Steve 'The Tarantula' Terisak. Steve was now "connected" to the Boston Mob and his parking attendant job was just a daytime legit cover.

He loved it and so did we. Anytime we introduced him to a lady we always used his nickname and woman would always say: "What an interesting nickname. How did you get that name?"

Steve would stand tall, tilt his shoulders back and say, "I'm connected." With that, a conversation ensued and Steve was "interesting." Even though he would always say that he could not discuss the origin of his name or what he did, that just added to the intrigue. We lost track of him over the years, but wish the old 'Tarantula' the best.

Meeting Checker:

One day as we curved the Frisbee in concert, Patty, a lady we knew from Phillips Street told us that for some reason she had been delivered mail addressed to Johnnie. Johnnie told her he would stop by later to pick it up. Patty was a great gal, not very ambitious, but really, none of us were back then. She was outgoing and always ready to party.

After dinner, Johnnie and I took a walk over to Patty's apartment to get his item of mail. We knocked and Patty opened the door. As we entered, we noticed this guy passed out on her coffee table. He was leaning off the edge of the couch with his head resting sideways on the coffee table and his arms hanging limp with his knuckles on the carpet. He was snoring. On the table were four empty GIQ's (giant imperial quarts) of Narragansett Ale and an ashtray with a stack of butts reaching to the sky forming a perfect pyramid. Patty was feeling little pain either.

"Hi Patty, we're here to pick up my mail. What's up with that guy?"

"Oh ... that's Checker. Would you like to meet him?"

"Sure." (This is going to be a good one, we thought.)

Patty brought us over by his side:

"Guys ... this is Checker."

She lifted the arm of his lifeless body into Johnnie's hand so he could shake his hand. Johnnie passed his limp arm to me. We tried not to laugh, but did not do a very good job. After shaking his hand I carefully returned his knuckles to the floor.

Patty gave Johnnie his mail, looked at us, and said:

"It's a good thing you met Checker now because he'd be in no shape to meet anyone when we get back from drinking tonight.

Last in the Line to Farm

The warm story of life on a farm.

Sioux Rapids, Iowa, along the Little Sioux River, is about as far away from the bright lights as you can get. Don't hold your breath for either Motley Crux, or any other Crux, to play this town anytime soon. Most folks wouldn't know who they are anyway.

But, none of this meant anything to Elmer Shank. Elmer was born here on a bone crunching cold January day in 1903. He was delivered by a neighbor, Hattie Lee Johnson. Little did Elmer Sr. and Sara know that their only son would love farming just as they did.

Life in Sioux Rapids was difficult in those days, even more difficult when you lived way outside town. The Shanks seldom got into Sioux Rapids except for church on Sundays, and once a month shopping at the General Store.

Little Elmer worked with his dad early on. When he was barely able to stand he was out working his assigned chores on the family farm that backed up to the river. Little Elmer loved the land. He was drawn to it. Right after breakfast he would rush outside to have the sun on his face and smell the sweet fragrance of the field with it's newly overturned soil. It was always windy and that suited Little Elmer just fine.

As Elmer grew up, farm life was all he knew. His friends in school talked all the time about graduating and leaving for the big city. Elmer had no such thoughts. He and his dad brought the corn crop in year after year. While they did not have dairy cattle, they did grow and sell hay. Even when Elmer's forearms were bright red and riddled with straw cuts from hay bales, he loved pitching the bales to the highest tier on the old hay wagon.

Elmer's mom had a big vegetable garden. Some say her beets were the sweetest around. The family sold corn, hay, and vegetables and made an honest living.

Elmer did well in school and attended many FFA classes. He played football and was a class officer. He dated Sue-Sue, but always spent as much time as he could out around the farm. Often he would hold on to the old wooden fence to support himself in the wind, close his eyes and enjoy the sweet smell of the field. He liked to walk out into the field and take an afternoon nap. He told his friends how special this was to him and they laughed and said he was nuts.

* * *

After Elmer graduated from high school, much of the farm work was his responsibility. His dad was getting on and less able to do most of the heavy chores. Elmer married Sue-Sue and soon little Jessica was born. Family life filled the old farmhouse.

Sundays were special. After church, and after a fried chicken dinner, they all gathered on the front porch and talked. Elmer would look out into the field and think back about his childhood.

"I wish I had a dollar for every time I ran out into that field."

As a youngster, Elmer competed every summer at the County Fair. His favorite event was the Tractor Driving Competition. His specialty event featured backing a manure spreader into a shed. There was a staked area, with driven wooden posts, that represented a parking shed for a manure spreader. The opening of the area was about six inches wider than the spreader. Contestants would have a one-axle manure spreader connected to a tractor of any size. The event called for the contestant to drive up past the shed, then back the spreader into the shed. The event was timed from when the contestant started to back up. If the contestant hit a pole, points were deducted. Each contestant had four tries. Every year, Elmer would come roaring up and back right into the shed clean with the winning time.

One winter, Elmer Sr., now 76, suffered a bad compound leg fracture. He had fallen off the tractor. The fracture was set, but they could not control an infection he developed and he died soon thereafter. Sara followed a few months later. The family suspected she died of melancholy. Elmer Sr. and Sara were buried behind the barn on a small hill overlooking the field. One Sunday, Elmer told Sue-Sue and Jessica that was where he wanted to be buried when his time arrived.

As the calendar pages flipped, and years passed, Elmer continued working the farm. Neither Sue-Sue nor Jessica embraced farm life. Sue-Sue did what she could with the garden. Elmer was able to boost corn yield and they managed financially. Jessica left for college, eventually got married, and moved to Grand Rapids with her husband. Soon after, Elmer, now 80, found the work on the farm difficult. Sue-Sue asked him to sell the farm so they could move into town. He wanted no part of it. Five years later, she tried again. The following year it didn't matter. She was buried on the hill. As she had requested, she faced away from the field.

Elmer kept on, but soon Jessica was asking him to either move in with her and her husband or go into an assisted living facility. Elmer was unable keep up and leased out his land. He spent most days on the front porch. He often looked back on his life. He wished the Lord had given him a son, but accepted what the Lord had given him. He was thankful for all the blessings he had received.

It was a cool fall morning when Elmer finished the breakfast dishes and went out on the porch for a spell. He looked out into the field through the mist and thought he saw a figure standing in the middle of the field. He could not make out the figure. He struggled to lift himself out of his chair and lumbered slowly out into the field. As he got closer to the figure, the figure seemed to be melting into the mist. He began to lose strength. Elmer lay down. He looked over toward the figure and it was not there. He felt a wonderful calm come over him. Elmer extended his arm out, grasp some sweet soil and brought it to his chest. It was then his eyelids gently closed.

The Powerful Force

Brut force meets a different powerful force.

Thousands of tourists have passed by the Arch of Constantine in Rome, Italy. Since it stands adjacent to the famous Coliseum, and is currently fenced in, it seems to get little attention. The arch was built in AD 315, commissioned by the Roman Senate in tribute to Roman Emperor Constantine's victory over the tyrant Maxentius at the Battle of Milvian Bridge. Constantine I, who ruled between 306 and 337 AD, proclaimed the Christian religion as the official religion of Rome.

If you look closely, you will notice several chiseled rectangular penetrations located unsymmetrically toward the top of the arch. Many have wondered what was the purpose of these penetrations.

The Vandals, led by King Genseric, had raped, enslaved, murdered, and pillaged their way through what is now France, Portugal, Northern Africa, Sicily, Naples, and were marching on the gates of Rome. History records that Pope Leo I met King Genseric at the gates of the city in 455 AD. The Pope pleaded for the lives of the citizens of Rome and the sanctity of the churches and other religious facilities. If left unharmed, the Pope pledged to identify the location of all the wealth in the city, including the churches, and open all areas for plunder.

*　*　*

Surprisingly, upon a discussion with his Soothsayer Gundthamund, King Genseric complied. Gundthamund had convinced the King that if they allowed the Roman city to continue in commerce, they could return in the near future and plunder it again.

His army destroyed much of the early Roman structures, statues, and gardens in Rome. They met their match, however, with the Arch of Constantine.

One warm night in Rome, Gundthamund had a nightmare. He dreamt that if the arch could not be toppled, the Vandals would disband forever. The next morning, he told King Genseric what he saw in the nightmare.

King Genseric was determined to topple the arch. The King told his son, Huneric, that he was to work on a plan to topple the arch and he must be successful. The arch was a Roman structure, but King Genseric did not realize that under Emperor Constantine, and Christianity, the three internal arches represented the Father, the Son, and the Holy Spirit.

Huneric ordered two penetrations be chiseled through the arch at the top. He ordered ten huge wooden logs be cut to the width of the arch in length. He commissioned three thousand five hundred feet of large chain. He configured four hundred horses into formation, six horses abreast, sixty-seven rows of horses in length. His soldiers built a platform at the back of the arch and raised the logs up and wrapped them in chains. They passed the huge chains through the penetrations and connected the chains to the horse formation.

On Huneric's command, his troops began whipping the horses and the huge length of chains slowly became taught. The horses groaned, stepping forward and sideways under the tremendous force of the formation.

"Beat them, beat them!" cried Huneric.

After two hours of pulling, and many lunges of the huge formation, the arch did not budge. Huneric lost one hundred seventy-five overworked horses and about that same amount were injured such that they had to be destroyed. Huneric decided to use more horses.

Huneric assembled a formation of one thousand six hundred horses. The formation, a column of six horses abreast, stretched over a quarter of a mile long. The formation was to pull at the sound of the goat horn.

* * *

Pope Leo I and his staff had learned about the second attempt to topple the arch and assembled on Palantine Hill, a ridge overlooking the Arch.

Huneric commanded the horn be blown. The horses and chain groaned under the pulling force of one thousand six hundred horses. A large cloud of dust encircled the formation. The groan of the horses was deafening. The arch still did not budge.

"Beat them, beat them, until no horse is standing," yelled Huneric.

He ran down the formation:

"Whip them, whip them raw."

The horses snorted for air within the heavy dust. Many horses stumbled under the pull of the heavy chains. Fallen horses were trampled by other horses.

Just then, at the back edge of the Arch, the soil began to loosen and the arch movement was impending.

The Pope, dressed in formal Cassock with red Mozzetta stood in front of his staff of cardinals and bishops. They were elegant in white, papal red, scarlet, and violet choir dress. Pope Leo stepped forward and thrust his papal staff high in the air toward the huge Arch. The crucifix at the top of the his staff glistened in the early morning sun.

"Behold the glory of the Father, the Son, and the Holy Spirit."

Humeric continued to scream at his troops and finally fell to the ground exhausted. His horses began dying in droves, the chain began to lose tension and the arch settled back.

As the dust settled, hundreds of horses lie dead or dying. The effort had failed. Humeric lie exhausted on the ground pounding his fist into the earth.

The Father, the Son, and the Holy Spirit stood intact ... just as they have to this very day.

King Genseric and his army returned to North Africa. He was succeeded and died some years later. Following his death his once great Vandal army began to falter, disbanded, and eventually fell under Roman rule.

The Right Coach

I wish Coach Thomas had been my coach in High School.

THE FOLLOWING IS AN INTERVIEW BETWEEN A HIGH SCHOOL football coach, Hank Thomas, and a local hometown sports reporter. The big game is this Friday night. The hometown Lincoln Lions oppose their perennial rival, the Capital Heights Bulldogs.

Wednesday afternoon: 09/20/1964
"Coach Thomas, the town is abuzz with Friday night's contest against Capitol Heights. They beat you soundly last year. What are your thoughts?"

"We're as ready as we're going to be. We don't coach revenge, but the kids have been looking forward to this game for a long time."

"What's wrong with the players wanting revenge."

"We don't want the kids to harbor any emotions other than playing and enjoying the game. These are young men. They are expected to respect the sport and those who play the sport. In addition, we must look at each game

71

uniquely. A season must be looked upon as a hurdler who must concentrate on each hurdle, one at a time."

"Come on coach, this town wants revenge."
"Well, if we win they will have their revenge and if that will make them happy, well, so be it. We work hard with our kids to make them realize that the joy of winning should never exceed the sting of a loss. Whether you win or lose, there is much to be learned and improved upon."

"After last years' loss to the Bulldogs, their coach said that your team didn't deserve to be on the field with his team."
"Yes, I do remember that statement in the paper the next day. I'm sorry the coach would make such a statement. You will not hear a statement like that from our staff, let alone me. Our kids played their hearts out that night. Our defense held them to seventy-eight yards rushing. Had we not fumbled late in the game we would have been *in* the game to the end. It's unfortunate that a mistake by one player can have a big impact, but that's all part of the game. We all learned from it. It's in the past and that's where mistakes should remain, replaced by lessons learned and improvements."

"The Bulldogs coach didn't even shake your hand when you extended it after the game."
"That also was unfortunate. I don't know what he was thinking. Win or lose, coaches should extend a firm handshake, make good eye contact, and exchange a few comforting words of sportsmanship."

72

"Coach, late in the game you sent in second and third string players. Why would you do that with the game on the line?"

"One reason kids want to play for this team and one of the reasons why we are successful every year is that we develop all our players, not just the better players. No one feels like a bench warmer and they all share the total team experience. We make mistakes but we all share in the experience. That's what a team is. We don't change our player rotation for any special game."

"Coach, we have heard that you benched our best running back for the big game Friday. Why did you do that?"

"We have confidential team rules. They are very simple, straightforward, with no room for misinterpretation. All our players agree that they understand these rules and corresponding penalties. They each sign an acceptance. When a player breeches a rule, they stand the penalty for that breech."

"Coach, just a few more questions. I was in the principals' office recently and noticed a list of exceptional students posted. I noticed that certain individuals had asterisks by their names denoting them as members of the football team. Why were only the football players marked as such?"

"Our school is molding the future citizens and workers of this country. Those on the list will be our truck drivers, nurses, policemen, our medical doctors, and engineers. My staff sees that the development of student athletes as a top team priority. I asked the principal to denote our players who have made the list for all to see. If you count the number of asterisks you will find it almost equals the number of players on our roster. My staff and I are extremely proud of their accomplishments."

"You must feel a great sense of reward when the kids win."

"I do, but my real reward is when I hear from a past player who is a productive member of society. He calls to thank me for the values our staff instilled in him and attributes his success to these values."

"Coach, I was in the Bulldogs locker room before they took the field last year. Coach 'Knuckles' Mason said:

> *'OK ... listen up. Last year we whipped their butts and I expect nothing less this year. A six pack for each injured Lion that doesn't return to the game and a case for a carry off.'*

"Coach Thomas, what are some of the things you say to your team before a game?"

"We talk about individual accountability. Each player must do their job. We talk about awareness of penalties and fumbles. I remind them that in football, just like life, there are three important principals: **sportsmanship, respect, and honor.**"

"Coach, I know when you were hired two seasons ago, many wondered whether you were the right coach. Win or lose, there's no question in my mind. Thanks Coach Thomas, and go Lions!"

Friday night: 09/22/1964 (post game)
Lions 31, Bulldogs 28. No significant injuries, either team.

The Rush Project

What is going on here? ... surprise!

LOCATION: Top Secret Pentagon Systems Lab 36, Washington, DC.
DATE: Friday, August 15, 1947
TIME: 0900 hours.
SPEAKER: Major General Earl Foster, US Army.

LADIES AND GENTLEMEN, THANK YOU FOR BEING HERE. I'M sorry that many of you were rushed to this meeting from all over the country, with little or no information. I apologize also for the thorough clearance procedures you have been subject to during the last twenty-four hours, but I can assure you the project you have been assembled for is of the utmost National importance.

Look around the room. You may recognize many of the people seated. Assembled here are five of the top architects and twelve of the top engineers in this country. All of you have been selected for this project because you are the best at what you do and we know you will meet the challenging task ahead of us. Major Gipper Wells will take over from here."

"Thank you, General Foster. Ladies and gentlemen, let's lay this right out on the table. We have been asked to design and assemble a fully sustainable observation module for up to five occupants. The complete specifications have been prepared for each of you to review following this meeting.

This module must be tested and on the loading dock, with installation and operation manuals included. This must be accomplished in five days. That's Tuesday, June 19, no later than 1400 hours."

A collective gasp erupts and it seems as if everyone is talking at the same time.

"Please, settle down. Lunch will be served shortly. I'd like to introduce Miss Thurston. She will answer any administrative and logistics questions you may have."

"After you have read the specifications, please break into appropriate groups, select lead specialists, and assemble your questions. The specifications have been gone over very carefully. Hopefully, there will be little or no technical questions. Please note any long lead purchase items. We have sourcing specialists, available twenty-four hours a day to ensure that all components are on site to support our schedule."

"Our current schedule is to have a conceptual design by this time tomorrow. The detail design is required two days later. You will have a full staff of engineering technicians at your disposal. We will meet later today at 1500 hours for questions. Needless to say, you will not be leaving the building until the project is complete. We will, however, cater to your every need. You may not have any outside contact accept with immediate family. Again ... this endeavor is Top Secret. Thank you for your time. I will see all of you at 1500 hours."

As the review of the specifications moves forward, the group members are beginning to sketch out concepts based on the specification interpretation. The architects work on the basic module concept with the structural engineers, while the electrical and mechanical engineers work on the power and system requirements for the operation of the module.

DATE: Friday, August 15, 1947.
TIME: 1500 hours.
SPEAKER: Major Gipper Wells, US Army.

"Ladies and Gentlemen, the floor is open for technical questions from the Lead Specialists. Let's hear from the module design specialist first."

"Yes, Dr. Carol Siuda, Senior Architect: Sir, the module external finish is specified to be an indoor paint. May we assume the module will never be subject to the elements?'

"Yes, that is correct."

"The occupant profile is stated as maximum height of 3' 7". Should we consider safety features for children?"

"Consider all safety considerations for any individual's no taller than 3' 7."

"Sir, the module will have two sinks, one enclosed shower, but no commode. Is this so?"

"Yes."

"The module features a pressure sealed pass-through unit. Should that be centered in the module wall to accommodate the specified occupants or an average size individual?"

"Specified occupant."

"Thank you, Major. You have answered my questions for now."

"Thank you, Ms. Siuda. Remember, your team must present your module concept at our meeting, tomorrow at 1100 hours."

"Will the Lead Specialist for power and systems please ask your questions?"

"Yes, I'm Dr. Jim Panzarella: Our power requirements are fully understood and will be incorporated. However, I do have several systems questions. The specification calls for a two-way, wall mounted, non-verbal communication screen. Sir, this is recent technology and certainly cannot be obtained in a few days."

"The screen was rush ordered weeks ago and is on-site. All of you will be given a parts list of typical system and architectural components, such as beds, linens, and electrical and other components that were anticipated based on the specification."

"Sir, the specification calls for a constant internal atmosphere of molecular hydrogen and helium. In addition, the sink will dispense liquid methane. May I ask just what kind of observation will be conducted in this module?"

"No. Are there any additional questions? Please have your group prepared to present your power and systems conceptual design at the meeting tomorrow at 1100 hours."

DATE: Saturday, August 16, 1947.
TIME: 1100 hours.
SPEAKER: Major Gipper Wells, US Army.

"Ladies and Gentlemen, please present your conceptual design for the module, modular power, operational systems, and test plans."

Both groups present their work. With few comments, Major Wells and his staff approve the conceptual design. The following two days the detail design takes place and fabrication of the module and assembly move forward co-incident with assembly of the module systems. Hundreds of technical and assembly staff work twenty-four hours a day to meet the schedule. The test plan is conducted without a hitch. The module and it's service components, and manuals are boxed up for shipping.

DATE: Tuesday, August 19, 1947
TIME: 1100 hours

Three hours before the deadline, the boxed components are under guard on the loading dock. Jed Phillips and Sticks Martin, government dockworkers, stand by.

"Say, Jed, did you get a look at the shipping tags on these boxes?"

"Why, no, what do they say?"

"The tags just say "Area 51."

The Secret

For the love of your neighbor.

WHY DID AN OLD MUTT ALWAYS COME TO THELMA'S front porch around midnight every night? Some thought it was because the dog liked to stretch out on the second porch step to catch the early morning sun. Maybe. But on rainy days he would be stretched out on the top step, just under the eave of the roof, where the sun didn't hit until afternoon. Anyway, he was always on Thelma's porch.

Thelma Thompson retired years ago, just after she lost her husband, Willy. Thelma used to be full of life and very friendly. However, after Willy died, she became a recluse. One thing she didn't need was some old mutt hanging around. Every morning she would pour a cup of coffee and come out on porch only to find the dog fast asleep on her steps.

"Git … I say git. Git on out of here."

The dog would jump up and go down the steps, stop, lift it's leg, then run off. Thelma often wondered, why does that mutt always come back.

"Howdy Thelma," said Lucy Wagner, her next-door neighbor.

Thelma just nodded briefly to acknowledge Lucy. Lucy and her daughter, Jaynie, would often talk about when Willy was alive. Willy would fix things for Lucy and many a time would sit out on the front porch playing his harmonica. Thelma and Willy would come over for dinner from time to time. They always asked Lucy and Jaynie over for Sunday dinner in the back yard. Thelma and Lucy would often play checkers together. But, all that went away when Willy passed.

The next morning, bright and early:

"Git ... I say git. Git on out of here."

Thelma spent most mornings just sitting on the front porch. Losing Willy tore at her very soul. There was not a day gone by that she didn't think about him and all that they had been through.

She recalled, way back, when Willy got a new job. He was so happy and they finally had some extra money at the end of the month. Then, she remembers, when he was laid off and the little extra they had went out the door.

Then there was her gall bladder operation. She thought she was going to die and Willy had her sons and all her friends come visit her at the hospital to try to convince her she was not going to die.

Shortly after that, both her sons got caught trying to rob a liquor store. That was seventeen years ago. They were sent to a correctional institute in Illinois. She would save up bus fare and visit them when she could.

Several years ago, Thelma took a free adult education class to learn how to use a computer keyboard, but once she left the class, she couldn't afford a keyboard or a computer.

"Git … I say git. Git on out of here."

The dog rushes off and almost runs over Jaynie.

"Miss Thelma, could I come up on the porch?" asked Jaynie.

"Come on up, child. Don't be bashful."

Thelma paused, then asked, "Little Jaynie … why do you expect this old dog is always on my porch?"

"It's a secret, Miss Thelma."

"Secret, secret. What are you talking about, child?"

"I don't know, but it's a secret."

The next morning, Thelma slowly opens the door as to not spill her coffee and there's the dog sound asleep. She decides to just sit and observe the dog. *He's a small dog, but boy! Can he saw the lumber*, she thought.

Just then the dog woke, sat up, but did not run. Thelma walked toward him and he did not budge.

"Git … I say git. Git on out of here."

The dog did not budge but looked back at her with a sad expression. Thelma moved closer. The dog extended it's leg and started licking a large laceration. Thelma bent down and petted the dog. She felt sorry for him. She would have never wanted harm to come to the dog. She went inside and got a bowl full of warm water, soap, washcloth, and towel. She began to wash the wound and the dog extended his leg out to assist her. After she washed the wound she put on some salve and a bandage.

During the following days, Thelma started feeding the dog. It did not leave her yard and would often lie down beside her chair.

One day, Lucy and Jaynie were looking over at Miss Thelma's house:

"Mommy, Mommy ... Miss Thelma is talking to the dog and the dog is laying beside her.

"Really ... that's wonderful, absolutely wonderful," said Lucy.

Soon the dog was on Thelma's lap. They were becoming fast friends. Thelma seemed to talk all day with the dog. She decided to call him "Sunrise" because that's the time of day she would find him on her steps.

Thelma seemed to be perking up.

"Lucy ... did you see my dog? He's fixed up. I named him "Sunrise," said Thelma.

"Why, yes. I'm so happy you have a little friend. Would you and Sunrise like to come over for Sunday dinner in our back yard? Say one o'clock?" asked Lucy.

"Sure. We'll come by right after I walk Sunrise."

That Sunday, family and friends gathered. It was a wonderful sunny day. Sunrise loved all the attention from the children.

"Little Jaynie. What was all that talk of a secret you mentioned a few weeks back?" asked Thelma.

Just then, Sunrise jumped up on Jaynie trying to lick her face.

"It's not important anymore," said Jaynie.

"It's not? Well, I'd still like to know the secret. Everyone likes to know secrets."

"Well ... OK, remember how everyone was wondering why the dog was always on your porch every morning?" explained Jaynie.

"Yes, dear. Yes, dear. What is the secret?"

"Well, my mom and I felt sorry for you that you had lost Willy and were alone. We noticed a stray dog on the street and encouraged it to visit you. Every night when mom came home from her late shift, after you had gone to bed, she would bring over a dish of dog food and a bowl of water. Then, early in the morning, before you got up, I would pick up the dishes and bring them back home. Mom and me were hoping you would take to the dog. Pretty good secret, huh, Miss Thelma?"

Three Oranges

Some things are not always as they seem.

ONE DAY I CAME ACROSS A SALE ON ORANGES AT MY LOCAL market. I don't usually eat oranges, but for a change, I bought three. I have to admit, I was looking forward to drinking the sweet juice. Coincidently, the neighbors three sons were expected for a family get together. I hope these oranges are better than those three kids were when they were young … I said to myself.

The silver spoon has never been shinier than next door at my neighbors. Ben Williams and his wife, Tracy, raised three boys. All three were spoiled rotten.

Ben was a very successful attorney in Atlanta, Georgia. So successful, that he worked twelve hours a day. Tracy was a CPA and worked less than Ben, but not much less. Their boys, then in high school, had lots of time on their hands and lots of money. I seldom saw them all together and never saw them go on a family trip or even the dad and sons playing catch. After high school, the three boys left home in different directions.

Ben, Jr., went to college in Charleston, South Carolina, but did not graduate. I remember when he would hop in his car when he lived at home. He would look into the rearview mirror and fuss with his hair for fifteen minutes before he would start the car up. I remember one summer day he pulled up in the driveway, flung open the door and threw the contents of his ashtray high with the wind. Most of his butts carried over into my rose bushes. I questioned him about it and he said:

"You must be mistaken. I don't do things like that."

One fall day, there were some workers from a landscape company raking leaves at the Williams's residence. When the workers formed a large pile of leaves, Ben came flying up on his bicycle and bust into the pile. He was warned to stop, but of course, did not. The workers stopped working and left.

Ben, Jr., came home last spring to visit. I ran into him as I was puttering out in front of my house.

"Well, hello there, Ben. I haven't seen you in maybe three years. What are you doing now?"

"Well, sir, I work for a brokerage firm."

'What do you do for them?"

"I push worthless penny stocks, wait until they go up a few cents, then I dump them. I'm making lots of money."

"Don't they call that deceptive practice Pump and Dump?" I asked.

Ben just lowered his head, turned, and walked toward his front door.

Jeffery, the youngest of the three, was always in trouble. I can't tell you how many times the police were standing on the Williams's front porch with Jeffery.

I guess he never did anything really bad. I heard it was usually just petty theft. One day I saw him back up his truck into the driveway. In the bed of the truck was what looked like sections of a birdbath. He unloaded the base and bowl out of his truck into a wheelbarrow and disappeared into the backyard.

About an hour later the police showed up. Back out came the wheelbarrow and its contents. I also ran into Jeffery recently:

"Hey, Jeffery, how are you doing?"

"Fine, Mr. Arlen. Sure feels good to be home."

"What have you been up to, Jeffery?"

"Well, if it wasn't for government programs and Mom and Dad I'd be in rough shape. I just can't seem to find a job."

Jessie, the youngest son, was the worst, I recall. Jessie had no respect for authority. One winter he laughed at me when I slipped on my icy driveway. It was a bad fall and I broke my kneecap. Instead of calling for medical assistance, he just laughed uncontrollably, got into his car and drove off.

Ben Sr. told me Jeffrey had attended college and graduated. He returned home often and I would go out of my way to avoid him. Last year, I was out by the rose bushes and Jessie rolled into the driveway.

"Mr. Arlen, gosh, it's been years. I'm glad I ran into you. I want to apologize for not helping you years ago when you fell in your driveway. Actually, I'm not all that proud of my behavior during those years before I left for college."

"Well, thank you, Jessie. What did you do after college?"

"I've been working with children with disabilities. I love my work as a physical therapist. It's very rewarding. Funny, you never know what life has in store for you."

"Jessie, I'm so happy you have a rewarding job."

"Thanks, my wife is expecting and we're very excited."

Later that day, I decided to eat one of the oranges that I had bought. They had sat on my kitchen counter for several days. I sliced it in quarters.

I could tell something was not right. The texture was very rough and the orange content was pale and not juicy at all. I bit into a slice and spit it out. It had little or no flavor.

About a week later I tried the second orange and it was just like the first. I kept putting off eating the third orange. Finally, after a week, I decided to give it the benefit of the doubt. I sliced into it. It was colorful and juicy. I ate the whole orange and enjoyed it thoroughly.

Truly, the Best of Friends

My description of a true story of friendship.

JOSEPH C. STEINWACHS, III, AKA 'STEINY OR THE KRAUT Boy,' was a remarkable character. He was fiercely independent, street smart, and had a quick wit. He was always there for his friends, especially to party. He had a fondness for the vices and served them well. Steiny was a proud Viet Nam veteran and a life member of the VFW. The Kraut Boy was long on relaxing and short on get up and go, but managed to make ends meet working as little as possible. When he worked, he worked hard.

I remember when he used to stop by the house with his ice cream truck. The truck had many dents and dings, lots of rust, and was plastered with funny bumper stickers. After he left from the front of my house, there was often an oil spill. I told him that every time he shows up at my house, the property value dropped. He always brought our dog, Peanut, a huge steer femur from a butcher he gave ice cream to.

Steiny and I had many adventures, but one night in particular stands out. Following an extended happy hour, we decided to stop by Billy Bob's to see Johnny Cash in concert. Billy Bob's is a huge country and western bar in

89

Fort Worth, Texas. When we found out how much the cover charge was, we decided to see if we could sneak in a back door. After trying several back doors, we found one that was open with no one there. Within a few lefts and rights, we entered the back of the stage area. To our surprise, there was Johnny and June Carter Cash and the band behind the closed curtains getting ready for their concert. We said "hi," wished them luck, and shook their hands. Then we took a stage right, down some stairs, out the door, and onto the main floor. Ahhhhh … the memories.

Ann Marsh was likable and attractive and worked for the local VFW as a bartender. Ann also had a fondness for the vices. She, too, just managed to make ends meet and lived in a small house in disrepair down a dusty dirt road.

Of course, in the small Texas town they lived in, it would not be long until they met. The VFW and alcohol brought them together. Both Steiny and Ann were fun and engaging people. Joe fell for Ann as soon as he saw her. They became fast friends.

Ann was truly just scraping by. Their friendship was rock solid. Steiny, also living day to day, could always find a few extra dollars to help her along. He paid many of her utility bills, and sometimes, her rent and car repair. Steiny was always a good tipper and especially so when Ann was working. He was at the VFW just about every night relaxing and talking with Ann every chance they got. Ann was very endeared to Steiny.

One warm summer Saturday afternoon, Ann stopped by the store and among other things bought two quick pick lottery tickets and went home, then into work. That night, the bar erupted when Ann had a winning ticket. It turned out that she ended up sharing the pot, some one hundred forty-four million, with another winner. Ann's world was turned upside down.

Ann quit work and bought a beautiful hilltop ranch just outside of town. She hired many of her friends, including Steiny, to work the ranch. She bought a herd of Long Horn cattle to roam the hillside. She was so happy. However, once drinking heavily with little money, she was now drinking heavily with lots of money. Before long, her friends, excluding Steiny, just sat around the pool drinking all day. Her best girlfriend was her business agent and bookkeeper. That same girlfriend's boyfriend was the ranch manager. Ann noticed that large sums of money were being paid to a company that was retained to do fence repair. She then discovered that her girlfriend owned the fence company and they were embezzling money from her.

Ann fired all her friends, except Steiny of course ... and sold the ranch. She began a darker stage of her life. She began regularly visiting Hawaii. She would rent an expensive oceanfront suite, close all the curtains, order a case of wine to be sent up to her room, and sit in the dark drinking alone. The hotel cleaning staff would not be allowed in to clean. After a period of time the hotel management would contact Steiny to come and get her. The hotel no longer wanted her as a guest. It was after one of these trips that Steiny helped her to realize what her life had become.

She met another man who also helped her to turn her life around. She and her new boyfriend opened up a Bed & Breakfast on Kauai. The business thrived, and so did Ann and her boyfriend.

Ann would fly Steiny over to Kauai often to visit and stay at the Bed and Breakfast. They all loved Hawaii. Steiny really enjoyed the lavish buffet dinners at local hotels and Ann and her boyfriend enjoyed their time with the old 'Kraut Boy.' They would often go to Polihale Beach, a wild, remote, beach on the western side of the island. It was their favorite beach.

*   *   *

Steiny had developed acid reflux problems late in life. One day, he was having trouble swallowing. He went to the hospital for an evaluation. They found that he was very ill and his prognosis was grim. Ann wanted to get him into the best treatment possible, but Steiny refused all treatment. He would go out his own way. He did fine for six months or so then he started failing. Ann had him flown to Kauai and got him into local medical treatment where she could visit him often. She eventually moved him into a facility.

Steiny died shortly thereafter. Ann discussed arrangements with his family and she had his body cremated. She and her boyfriend spread his ashes into the surf at the beach he loved.

They were truly the Best of Friends.

Two Days in Hell

The reality of war.

ONE DAY AN OLD BLACK DOG WALKED INTO NED WEB-ster's heart in 1860. Backwoods Illinois was a lonely place back then, but not for Ned after Blackie showed up. Blackie had a mind of her own. She was faithful, not to any cause, but to those who pursued one. He had wanted to give the dog a name, but by then he was so busy he just kept calling her Ole Blackie. Now there was no time for such thing.

In August of 1861 Ned was called by his country. He and Blackie formed up with his neighbors, William Mc-Clinton, and T 'Hoots' Hatch. Soon, they said goodbye to kinfolk and started down many a dusty road to form up with the 34th Illinois Infantry Regiment, Company A, the 'Rock River Rifles,' at Camp Butler, just northwest of Springfield.

Ned had strapped an old knapsack to Blackie's back. The knapsack carried hard tack, bandages, extra brown sugar, matches, candles, and such. During training at Camp Butler, Blackie would dart between the half tents visiting all the men. Soon, different recruits were sending notes and trading various items. She was liked by all.

About the same time, Samuel Waits and his buddies W.T. Potsworth, J. McWenty, and Thomas Kist answered their call by their country and enlisted in the 17th Alabama Infantry Regiment, Company C, in Montgomery, Alabama.

Among other Regiments, the 34th Illinois and the 17th Alabama would stand their first fight on April 6th & 7th of 1862, at the Battle of Shiloh, also known as Pittsburg Landing.

The southern forces were commanded by General Albert S. Johnston. On the 6th, Sunday, General Johnston's forces charged the Federal encampment, commanded General Ulysses S. Grant's forces. Johnston's men, took the day, and pushed the Union forces back to a defensive position, a sunken road, referred to as the "Hornets Nest" near the banks of the Tennessee River. That's what the history books will tell you. Seldom discussed, however, lost in between the lines of historical text, is the horror that accompanied the day.

Both regiments were trained, but the training could never prepare them for heat, sweat, dust, screams, tears, smoke, and agony that took place that day. The best of situations was to make it through the day. Ned lost track of Blackie in the smoke and dust. William McClinton, his neighbor, went missing, and 'Hoots' did not make it. A rebel bullet found an artery in his leg and he slowing bled to death screaming for help. His screams were lost in the many screams of the day ... all of them terrifying.

Never in his life had Ned seen such carnage. His unit was taught to fight in ranks and what he managed to live through was complete disarray and panic. No ranks, just murderous brutality, he thought. He had lost the two friends he had enlisted with:

"Father forgive me for my harvest today, comfort their families, bless their children. Bless and keep 'Hoots' and William," he prayed.

Ned was physically and emotionally exhausted and confused. All of a sudden, Ole Blackie appeared out of nowhere. "Thank you, Father," Ned said. Blackie didn't stay long. Against Ned's wishes, she dashed across the field and disappeared within the Rebel ranks.

Samuel Waits and his buddies in the Southern ranks, had all the fight they wanted too. W.T. Potsworth died that day. A bayonet emerged from the thick cannon smoke, plunged deep into his chest, and ended his dream of becoming a master cabinetmaker. Thomas Kist was taken prisoner, never to be seen again. Samuel Waits and J. McWenty lay low in the tall grass stunned by what they had witnessed. Samuel whispered:

"Fightin' ... Fightin.' Hell, I could hardly see. My eyes are still burning from the dust, sweat, and smoke. Screaming, screaming. My God ... make the screaming stop! I never thought war had such a sweaty stench. I never thought there was so much anger in Kill in.' I thought it was going to be like paint n' fence pickets: finish off one and move on to the next."

"Well, it kinda' is," said McWenty. "You keep on until you either run out of paint or run out of pickets."

They welcomed the quiet of the evening, and the blanket of mist and darkness of the evening.

Monday, the 7th, Ned woke up in the Union encampment with Ole Blackie snuggled against him.

"Form up ... form up," shouted Captain H.W. Bristol.

A moan from the encampment ensued.

Across the field, Samuel Waits and J. McWenty readied for battle preferring to stay busy rather than taking time to reflect. The ranks were quiet.

"You ready, J? It's fightin', just fightin', plain and simple," said Samuel.

Over the battlefield an uneasy calm prevailed. Soon the peaceful mist covered field would be turned into a blood soaked hell as the wheat met the scythe in the name of honor and country. The reinforced Union Army of the Tennessee managed a successful charge late in the day that inflicted heavy casualties and forced the Rebels into retreat. The losses of the previous day were avenged.

However, lost in the Union victory, was the price paid by both sides. Ned struggled to assist a comrade. As he was dragging him off the field, he was shot in the head and died instantly. Ole Blackie, struck by a random bullet, lie in agony on her side, constantly yelping and moving to try to lessen her pain. A fallen soldier lying closely pulled his revolver and ended Blackie's misery. The weakened soldier could have shot at the enemy, but decided he had enough of killin'. Another fallen man lying adjacent to Blackie raised an arm up to the heavens and mumbled something then his arm fell lifelessly upon Blackie's breast.

As the battle raged, Samuel Waits, gut shot, lay on his side. Somehow he was totally relaxed, oblivious to what was going on around him, and his fate. His eyes were burning and his vision was blurry from rolling sweat. Through the sickening fog of war he saw men in death struggles. At their feet lie hundreds of fallen soldiers, butternut and blue alike, lying still or writhing in agony. He struggled to raise his canteen to his mouth to savor the cool water, then promptly was shot behind his ear. His arm fell limp and the contents of his canteen spilled, turning pink, as it mixed with the blood soaked meadow.

J. McWenty was wounded but survived the day, only to fall several years later at Oostenaula Bridge, near Resaca, Georgia.

* * *

Some 23,000 men died during the two days of fighting. These heroes, both blue and gray, were fighting for their vision of freedom. They joined the cause for that vision. They stepped up to battle formation for their families, fellow soldiers, and their states, and they stepped off into the fight for their lives.

Exodus

An exodus by any other name is still an Exodus.

PROFESSOR WARREN HESTER OF WESTWOOD UNIVERSITY IS well known in the world of Egyptology. He has been the Chair of the Ancient Egypt Studies Department for the last three decades. If there was an important expedition in Egypt, he had something to do with it. He had led numerous worldwide research excavations himself.

El Habeen Kalid is the Minister of Antiquities for the country of Egypt. Like Professor Hester, Kalid is well known, and the two have worked together in the past on many important projects.

"Professor Hester, this is El Habeen."

"My God, how long has it been? I was thinking of you, recently. A student of mine has just finished an interesting paper entitled *Practical Methods of Artifact Preservation*. I wanted you to see it."

"I'd like to see it, sir. Professor, I just had to call you. We have identified a very promising large dispersion of early Egyptian war artifacts."

"Where are these artifacts located?"

"Are you sitting down, Professor?"

"Yes, I am, and very interested."

"Just south of Ismailia, not far from Lake Timsah."

"I don't recall any major Egyptian battles in that region. Wait a minute, wait a minute! Do you think these artifacts could possibly be associated with the Exodus? While remote, that has been identified as a possible route. My God, what a huge biblical find this would be."

"Yes, Professor, it is a remote possibility. I must ask you to keep this very quiet. You can imagine the implications. The artifact field seems to be very large. Two workers, taking water samples within a one thousand square foot grid found two partial chariot wheels, a shield, and several spears. These artifacts were about three feet under the silt. As soon as I heard of this, I thought of you. Because of the sensitivity of this matter, there will be no general request for proposals. We need you to assemble a small staff and map the artifact debris field for possible excavation. The work will be funded by the General Antiquities Fund. I will sign it off."

"Professor, I need to discuss recent developments concerning antiquities projects. The Egyptian Parliament has passed sweeping legal changes concerning exploration and research projects in Egypt. I'll be sending you all this information, but I wanted to run several important features to you. Parliament has appointed a new department, a watchdog group really. As you know, many exploration groups have not honored their commitment to return search areas to the pre-dig natural setting. A $500,000 deposit is now required prior to any approved exploration or excavation. There are other stipulations, but they are minor. I'll get the complete project specification to you shortly."

"El Habeem, thank you so much for the honor of working on this project. You can be sure the location and project plan will not be divulged. My team will be given the minimum information."

Professor Hester evaluates the specification and instructs his team based on need-to-know. He can hardly control his emotions with the remote possibility that they may be cataloging artifacts in the very location of the Exodus. The professor calls the Minister of Antiquities:

"El Habeem, we are comfortable with the project specification. We have met the financial and technical requirements and are raring to get started."

"OK, thanks, Dr. Hester. As soon as we are in receipt of all the required documents and deposit, I'll be back to you. I'm just as anxious as you are."

Several weeks later, El Habeem calls Professor Hester with the good news. The first phase will be a familiarization of the site, a discussion about hiring of local workers, and general implementation of the project. El Habeem tells the professor that he will not be able to attend this meeting. His assistant Tomar Azir, will meet with his team.

The professor and his project managers fly into a local airport in Ismalia and meet Tomar Azir as planned:

"Mr. Azir. We are pleased to meet you and anxious to begin this exciting project."

"It is certainly nice to meet you, sir. El Habeem has often spoken highly of you. When will we be going to the debris site?"

"What site are you referring to? El Habeem told me you were coming to present a paper concerning the practical methods of preservation of artifacts."

"What? Let's get El Habeem on the phone."

"I'm sorry, Professor. El Habeem retired somewhere in France three weeks ago."

"What! We transferred $500,000 into an account given to us by El Habeem for this project."

Flying Death

Better know who your friends are.

A MAN SITS ON A SUN-LIT PARK BENCH IN BOSTON COM-mon. He is reading a newspaper and waiting for someone to ask where a hat shop is. He has a lunch pail on the ground between his legs. A women sits down but says nothing and soon leaves. Shortly thereafter, an older man sits down. After a few minutes he reaches into his pocket, pulls out a sandwich, and takes a bite. He turns to the other man and says:

"Excuse me, sir. Do you know where I can find a hat shop?"

"No, but I believe we have an event to discuss. My hatred of an individual brings me to you. I understand you are very good at what you do and very thorough. Would you explain how you conduct an event?" asks the first man.

Vinnie sneezed. "I do an event study and complete the event within a week."

"Look," said the first man. "I'm really concerned about the event coming off clean, no mistakes. No one must know."

"Don't be concerned. You are talking with me because I'm the best at what I do. During the implementation of the event, I will be miles away. I promise you, no one will ever know about this."

"How will you take care of this guy?"

"I don't discuss events until they are completed. I do a post event evaluation with my clients. I will explain the details of the event at that time."

"Here's a picture of him along with his address. This lunch pail contains the $13,800 cash, paid in full, as you requested."

Vinnie looks at the picture, and says, "Let's see, today is Saturday. Meet me here a week from today at exactly 2p.m."

The first man walks off. Vinnie empties the cash from the lunch pail into his pants and coat pockets and begins to examine the lunch pail. Just as he thought, stuffed into the pail handle, hidden, is a small transmitter. He leaves the pail on the park bench and on his way home deposits the cash immediately distributed between six banks, in unequal amounts.

The following morning Vinnie begins surveillance of the event subject. The subject makes short trips from his house numerous times over the weekend. Vinnie also notices that everyday, around 1p.m., the subject walks down Charles Street to a small sandwich shop for lunch. His walk down Charles Street takes approximately seven minutes.

Back in his apartment, Vinnie inserts a tiny powder charge into a small aircraft drone and completes the wiring. He packs the drone into a suitcase.

Friday morning he takes his drone outside the city to a secluded field. At 12:45p.m. he deploys the drone, at 1:08p.m. the drone is traveling above Charles Street and losing altitude. Using visual, Vinnie locks the laser on the subject's upper body. At 1:09p.m. the subject is terminated.

Saturday, 6p.m., Channel 4 Action News:

"A South Boston man was killed in Boston Common about 2p.m. today. Witnesses said the man, sitting on a park bench, was struck from behind by a flying drone that exploded on impact. No other people were injured. Police officials don't believe this was an accident and believe this killing may be related to a similar killing on Friday. Currently, there are no suspects in either incident."

Charlotte's Wish

A Christmas wish comes true.

GRAMPY LEE IS SPENDING CHRISTMAS WITH HIS SONS IN California. He lost his wife, Judy, several years before, and is looking forward to a family Christmas. He is staying with his youngest son, Andy, his wife, Jana, and their children, Charlotte and Oliver. Charlotte is three, Oliver, almost one. Grampy's oldest son, Donald, and his girlfriend, Yadira, will also be at Andy's for the celebration. It's Christmas Eve:

"Charlotte ... would you like Grampy to read you a story?"

Charlotte, all excited, is jumping up and down on her tip toes:

"Yes, Grampy, yes, yes. I'll be right back. I'll get a book."

Grampy looks across the room and is looking at the large snowflakes falling beneath the street light. How mesmerizing and peaceful. Ever since he was a kid he loved looking at falling snow.

"Grampy ... here's a book. It's called *Rebecca's Wish*. Uncle Donald read it to me not long ago."

"OK ... hop up on Grampy's lap and we'll get started."

"It was a dark, cold night and Rebecca decided that tonight was the night she would make her wish. She pulled her covers tightly around her and started saying her prayers. At the end of her prayers she started her wish: Father ..."

Charlotte, interrupting: "Grampy, do you believe in wishes?"

"Why, yes, I do, Charlotte."

"Me too, Grampy. I ask Jesus to listen to my wishes. Do you ask Jesus to listen to your wishes?

"Yes, I do. I certainly do."

"If you were to ask for a wish right now what would it be, Grampy?"

"Well, let's see. I miss your Nana, dearly. I miss Christmases past with her and your dad when he was a boy, and, of course, your Uncle Donald. They were always so excited, especially on Christmas morning, just like you and Oliver will be."

Charlotte snuggled deep into Grampy's cradled arm.

"Did you say something, Charlotte?"

"Ah, no, Grampy."

Grampy read for what seemed like hours. It was not long before they were both sound asleep and dreaming ...

* * *

"Don ... are you going to stare out that window at the snow all day?"

"I'm sorry, Judy. I'll get some more firewood in. It will be nice to have a cozy fire for Christmas Eve."

"Yeh, Dad, I love a big fire. Hey, Donald, quit tapping on that," said Andy.

"Oh, shut up! Go suck on a plastic bag," said Donald.

"That's enough you kids. It's Christmas. Let's all get along. Dinner is going to be ready soon. Everyone get washed up," said Judy.

"Donald, come with me. I need someone to hold the door open for me when I bring in the firewood," said Don.

Donald opened the door and Don came rushing through with a large armload of firewood. "Man, it's cold out there. Thanks, Donald."

They all sat down for Christmas Eve dinner. The dinner was a Lee family traditional of spaghetti and meatballs with antipasto salad and garlic bread. Every year Don made a rum cake from scratch that everyone loved. Don always loved this dinner, even though it took forever to help clean up.

After dinner, they assembled in the living room with all the house lights off except the Christmas tree. The glow of the tree lit up the presents beneath. The kids were not allowed to be near the presents until Christmas Eve just before they went to bed.

"OK, kids ... go look at the presents. It's bedtime soon," said Judy with a wonderful holiday spirit in her voice.

Donald and Andy raced over to the base of the tree and began rummaging through the presents.

"Go easy over there."

"Hey, Donald ... this one is for you, it's big. I wonder what it is?"

Dad said, "Well, you'll have to wait until tomorrow."

"Andy, do you want to put out the cookies and milk for Santa this year?" said Judy.

"Yeh! Thanks, Mom."

"OK, let's do that. Then you guys need to be off to the sack. We have a long day tomorrow."

Don goes over to the tree and straightens out some of the presents then reaches up on the tree to adjust some lights. The kids rush up the stairs and are in for the night. Judy looks warmly at the beautiful tree:

"Don ... I think this is the most beautiful tree we have ever had."

Don draws her near and embraces her:

"We are so fortunate for what we have and I am so lucky to have you as my wife. I love you, Judy."

"I love you too, Don, and I will always love you."

"Let's get Santa's presents for the kids. Where did you hide them this year? asked Don.

"They're inside the big ottoman in the den. I know the kids would never have thought to look in there," said Judy.

They rush into the den and bring the extra presents to put under the tree.

"Judy, can you hold the back door for me. I have to bring in Donald's bike. It's in the trunk of my car."

Once everything is under the tree, they embrace.

"Let's hit the sack. I'm ready for some dancing sugar plums," said Don.

"Me, too. Santa ... don't forget to eat a cookie or two and drink some milk. Don't eat all the cookies!"

Zero dark-thirty the next day ... Christmas morning:

"Donald, Donald ... get up, lets go."

The kids rush downstairs and marvel at what Santa has brought and rush upstairs to tell their mom and dad.

"Mom ... come quick! Santa brought us even more stuff. He even ate some cookies while he was here."

Mom and Dad get out of bed and soon all are gathered around the tree. Donald is sitting on his bike and aglow with excitement. Andy is tearing a present open. Donald races over and slides along the carpet until he comes to rest beside a pile of presents.

"Now, read the tags please. You will be writing thank you notes."

"Ah ... do we have to?" said Donald.

"Don, this one is for you."

"Oh ... OK, thanks, dear." He reaches into the base of the tree.

"Here's my present to you, Judy."

She opens the present.

"Oh ... Don, this is just the sweater I wanted. How did you know about this?"

"Donald told me all about it. Remember when you took him shopping with you? You stopped and looked at the sweater and held it up to yourself. Donald described the sweater to me."

Judy starts laughing. "Yes ... I remember, but Don, it was expensive."

"Nothing is too expensive for my Judy."

Before long, the floor is covered with wrapping and the kids are playing with all the new toys.

"Don, this is a wonderful Christmas. We are blessed."

"We truly are, dear."

*　*　*

Grampy, Grampy ... wake up!

"Oh, I'm sorry dear. I guess I dozed off. Charlotte, I had the most wonderful Christmas dream. It was my exact wish: The wish I told you about.

"Then my wish came true, Grampy," said Charlotte.

"It did, what did you wish for, Charlotte?"

"I wished that your wish would come true."

"Thank you, dear. Let's go out and give your mom and dad a big hug and thank them for a wonderful family Christmas."

Guests of John and Mable

A whimsical tale set at the Ringling Museum, Sarasota, Florida.

THE RINGLING MUSEUM IN SARASOTA, FLORIDA, IS AN amazing and whimsical place. The crown jewel of the beautiful grounds is Ca' d' Zan, or "House of John." This opulent palace on Sarasota Bay, was the winter residence of John and Mable Ringling, of circus and real estate development fame. Their home has a timeless elegance. Mable passed away in 1929, shortly after the residence was completed. Upon John's passing, in 1936, the house and grounds were given by them to the people of Florida. John and Mable were highly regarded and gave generously to charity.

Along with Ca'd'Zan, the sixty-six acre compound has several circus museum buildings, an art museum, and many gardens and groves of tropical trees and shrubs. The internment of John and Mable are adjacent to the Secret Garden. There are many small cherub statues on the grounds. The cherub statue entangled in banyan arterial roots mentioned in this story actually exists on the grounds. Have fun finding it when you visit.

"Excuse me, sir. Is it true that the admission to just the grounds is free today?"

"Why, yes it is. Are you college students? With a valid student ID card, full admission is just two dollars."

"Yes, we are. Sandra goes to Chamberlain School of Retailing and I go to the University of Buffalo, 'Go Bulls!' Since it's late in the day, could we both get in for two dollars?"

"No, I'm sorry."

"Well, we need our money for food so we'll be thankful to just walk the grounds."

Carl Zander and Sandra Alteri were lovers and traveling companions during the summer of 1966. They both had bedrolls and small backpacks. They travelled light, as light as possible. The canopy of their bed was often a blanket of stars.

"Sandra, I've got a dollar seventy-five. Maybe that's enough for a can of soda pop to share?"

Demetrious, a security guard, heard their conversation, and added:

"I'll throw in three dollars to help with your drinks. I'm sure you will find the grounds to be very special. Don't forget the grounds map. You two have fun out there."

"Thank you, sir."

Carl and Sandra set out and soon are in Mable's Rose Garden. They are taken by the spectacular variety of roses and statues.

Next they wind through a forest of ariel roots of a huge Banyan Tree. They emerge to see the striking Ca'd'Zan in the distance.

"Sandra, do you see that top tower of the building? That's called the Belvedere. Do you see the light pendant hanging way up there from the ceiling? I read that the Ringlings would turn that light on so their neighbors would know when they were at the estate.

They continue toward Ca'd'Zan and decide to visit the Secret Garden first.

John and Mable's neighbors and other friends gave them the special flowers and plants that make up The Secret Garden. This beautiful garden leads to the couples resting place.

As Sandra and Carl walk over to the Ringling gravesite, a cool breeze passes.

"Carl, let's say a silent prayer for John and Mable. They gave this wonderful treasure to the people of Florida. It's strange, but I feel very comfortable here. After our prayer, let's lie down under that banyan tree for a nap. I feel very sleepy."

Three hours later, they awaken to find it's almost dark and realize the park has closed. They walk out onto the walkway and see no one.

"Carl, what are we going to do?"

"Well, we can eat our oranges and that cheese we have, then hit the sack right under this banyan tree. In the morning, we'll just blend in with the crowd and go on our way. I love this place, I'll sleep like a log."

Just then within the large mass of aerial roots, a wind song:

"Come stay with us in Ca'd'Zan."

"Did you hear that! Did you hear that, Carl?"

"Hear what?"

"Listen."

"Come stay with us in Ca'd'Zan."

The wind song repeats. The couple searches the many tentacle aerial roots and come across a cherub statue on a pedestal wrapped in a cluster of aerial roots. The cherub utters:

"Come stay with us in Ca'd'Zan. The Tower Bedroom awaits you tonight."

"Carl … how can this be? Are the Ringling's asking us to stay with them?"

"This is unbelievable, but there is a 'Tower Bedroom' on the fourth floor of the mansion. I saw it on the floor layout. Let's go see if we can get into Ca'd'Zan," said Carl.

"Are you crazy, Carl? There must be all sorts of security around here, especially with the museum closed. As soon as we emerge from these ariel roots we'll be on a security camera or picked up by motion and sound sensors."

"Do you think John and Mable would ask us to stay with them if they knew we would be arrested for trespassing?"

"Well, it's crazy, but you have a point."

The couple embraces, turn, and walk toward the mansion. It is dark now.

"Oh my God. Carl, look up into the tower. The light is on."

As they approach the mansion on the walkway, a security guard approaches in the opposite direction.

"What do we do now, Carl?"

"Just keep walking, Sandra."

The guard is walking straight toward them and Carl and Sandra separate to allow the guard to pass between them. The guard says nothing and makes no eye contact.

"Can you believe that, Carl?"

The couple walk up to the solarium entrance. As Carl reaches for the doorknob, the door slowly opens to the young couple. There is a collective gasp as an impeccably dressed butler stands before them.

"*Welcome to Ca'd'Zan. The Ringling's will receive you shortly. Please sit here.*" Candles magically light as they are seated.

* * *

"Carl, look at this wavy window glass. This is one of the most beautiful rooms I have ever seen."

"The Ringling's will see you now. Please follow me."

The butler escorts the couple into The Court, the large living room, facing Sarasota Bay. They marvel at the tapestry's, opulent furniture, vases, chandeliers, and fresh cut flowers.

A piano player appears, his white gloved hands glide high above the keys and his music fills the room. They sit together on a raspberry color velvet couch.

"Wow, Carl, what a timeless charm this palace has," exclaimed Sandra.

In front of the couch is a multicolored marble table. Centered on the table is a large ornate glass fruit bowl, full of fresh fruit. At each end of the bowl are glass seahorses. Adjacent, on both sides of the fruit bowl are matching glass candle candelabras, with seahorses on both sides of the candelabra. The glass setting is stunning. The candles magically light and glisten.

Just then, John and Mable enter. Mable is elegantly dressed in a ruffled white blouse with a seahorse stickpin and brown skirt. John is wearing a collarless white linen shirt and light brown slacks with dark brown stripes. He is wearing silver cufflinks in the shape of elephants.

"John and I are so happy to have you as our guest tonight. You see, we relate to young lovers, even though we met later in life. We know you are respectful, and truly appreciate our home and grounds."

"Mrs. Ringling, we are overwhelmed by your hospitality and frankly, rather consumed with this whimsical experience. You both are so elegantly dressed, we feel out of place," said Sandra.

"You are college students and dressed appropriately. Please join us in a glass of wine."

The four chat, sipping Cabernet Sauvignon. An hour seems to fly by.

"Ladies and gentlemen, dinner is served," announced the butler.

They dine on a roast of beef with sauce béarnaise, steaming rice, and fresh sliced carrots. Mable and Sandra talk about the origin and variety of roses in Mabel's Rose Garden and Carl listens intently as John tells his favorite circus stories. Coffee and pineapple upside down cake finish the elegant dinner.

"I'm sorry we must go now," said Mable. *"We must return to our Father's mansion. The butler will show you to the Tower Bedroom and tend to your every need. It's been a pleasure to have you as our guests."*

"Thank you both so much for the wonderful magical night. We will always cherish your hospitality and this wondrous experience. We will always believe in the whimsical and magical." exclaims Carl.

The butler escorts the couple to the Tower Bedroom. Before they retire they climb the spiral stairs to the Belvedere. The moonlight shines on the beautiful glazed tiles, some with zodiac signs. As they are star gazing, the pendant light goes out. They retire.

"Sandra, Sandra, wake up. We need to go."

They leave Ca'd'Zan and return to the base of the banyan tree to await the opening of the grounds. Under the banyan tree, they visit the cherub. Shortly after the grounds opening, they returned to John and Mable's gravesite and thank John and Mable again for their hospitality. Carl turns to Sandra and they take each other's hands,

"Sandra, I can't explain what we have been through. I think people will think we are crazy if we relate this experience. But, I love you Sandra, and want you to be my wife."

"Oh, Carl, I accept. I will always cherish these two days with you and the Ringlings. Promise me we will come back here some day."

"You have my word, Sandra."

As they are walking up toward the Admissions Building, they run into Demetrious, the security guard:

"Hi folks, back again I see. There's so much to see here. Where did you guys put up last night? I know you could not have slept here on the grounds. This place has more security than the White House. Especially inside and outside of Ca'd'Zan."

Carl laughed and said, "We were guests of a very special couple."

LAX Gate 68C

A gate that only certain people may see.

EVER NOTICE GATE 68C AT LOS ANGELES INTERNATIONAL Airport (LAX)? Go down to the very end of the Delta terminal and look again. It's there, but most everyone cannot see it. That is, until it's time … their time. There's no aircraft at the end of the gate, but those who pass through Gate 68C do not return through this or any other gate.

Richard Allen never thought twice about Gate 68C at LAX. Every other Monday for the last thirteen years he flew out of Gate 68A to Miami on business. When he returned it was to either Gate 68A or 68B.

Richard was in his late sixty's and feeling every bit of it. He has been thinking of asking his boss about sending someone else on these taxing business trips, but he is worried about losing his job. Stick it out, he thought.

One Monday morning, he was sitting in the gate area and looked up and noticed Gate 68C. He wondered how the gate could have been constructed so quickly because he didn't notice it when he and his wife flew to Las Vegas for a vacation the week before. He turned to a passenger sitting nearby that he had often seen in the gate area:

"Excuse me, sir. Did you notice the new gate?"

"What new gate are you referring to?"

"That gate, 68C."

"I'm sorry, I don't see a Gate 68C. Are you sure you don't mean 68A or B?"

"No, 68C, it's right there. The one with no gate desk."

"I'm sorry, sir, but I do not see the gate."

The passenger gets up and moves a few rows over. Richard asks several other passengers and all deny the existence of the gate. Richard gets up and walks over to the gate. Just then he hears a voice:

Richard ... The gate has been identified only to you. Do not attempt to enter the gate.

Undaunted, he attempts to pass through but is stopped by the solid wall. He turns around and is embarrassed to find seated passengers who are wondering why he walked into a wall. Richard returns to a seat disillusioned and concerned. He tells his wife about the incident and she tells him he needs another vacation.

The following Tuesday, Richard returns to Los Angeles. His plane pulls up to Gate 68A and Richard walks slowly up the gangway. As he leaves the gate entrance he glances over and sure enough, there is Gate 68C.

Richard. Did you have a good trip?

Richard turns toward the voice. A little boy is standing there.

"Why, yes, yes, I did. Tell me little boy, would you point to Gate 68C. I can't quite make it out?"

The little boy points directly to the gate. Richard is taken back.

"Would you walk me over to the gate?" said Richard.

Sure. But, please do not try to pass through the gate, said the little boy.

As they walk toward the gate Richard is frightened to see that the boy walks right through other people to get to the gate.

Richard. Please go about your business. Do not fear. There are very good things in store for you.

Richard visits his pastor and tells him the entire story. The pastor raises his hands to his face and begins rubbing his eyes. He sighs, and then looks intently at Richard:

"Richard, I believe an angel has spoken with you. I know you are saved and you have been a tireless servant of this church. A tree is known by it's fruit and so will you be known. I'm sure the angel spoke the truth that very good things are in store for you."

Later that day before dinner, Richard's wife, Winny, offers a suggestion:

"Richard, you really must just forget about this gate thing. Let's go out tonight and have a nice quiet dinner. You are just tired and confused. A night out will calm you."

"Alright, Winny."

At dinner, Richard tells Winny what the pastor had told him.

"Richard, the pastor is just consoling you. You don't really think an angel talked with you, do you?"

"Why, yes, Winny, I do. You see, when you believe, your belief must be unconditional."

"Richard, believe, believe in what?"

Later that evening Richard was relaxing by the TV. He decided that in the end nothing's really important except God's love. He raised the recliner footstool up and sank deep into the recliner cavity. He rested his eyes. He awoke to find himself in front of Gate 68C with the little boy at his side.

Take my hand, Richard. There are very good things in store for you.

Richard and the little boy walked through Gate 68C.

Lost

The evil Captain Ismis meets his watery demise.

A T THE END OF THE FLORIDA MAINLAND THERE IS A LONG causeway that takes you to the northern end of Key Largo. The last segment of the causeway bridge passes above a small oval shaped bay, now called Lake Surprise. The highway splits the bay, east and west. Mangroves bound the bay. If you watch in the westerly direction as you pass overhead of the bay into Key Largo, you will notice, only for a few seconds, a secret passageway cut into the mangroves at an angle. In 1735, long before there was a road, bridge, or any land development, the area was visited by Captain Carl Ismis, his band of misfits, and their pirate ship: *The Sea Scorpion*.

Ismis was as ruthless as they come. His beady eyes were said to look right through ten men. Under duress, he spoke, but before he was answered, he shot or stabbed the individual. Then he answered his own question the way he wanted it answered. His ship was the most sought after pirate ship by the local authorities.

He and his crew had recently pillaged *The Sovereign Princess*, a British sixth-rate frigate, sailing out of the Dry Tortugas. They looted like vultures at a carcass stripping the crew and cargo, then setting the ship ablaze leaving those onboard to perish. The booty consisted of weapons, powder, food, rum, silver and gold, jewelry, a large hoard of Britain sovereign coins, and silverware. This treasure along with similar booty from the raiding of the Windsong, a ship full of passengers on a retreat, filled three large chests. Captain Carl did not want to lose these chests. In September he decided he would head for his favorite hiding place, the mangrove bay (Lake Surprise) in Key Largo.

The Sea Scorpion listed toward starboard and was slashed through the quiet seas of what is now Blackwater Bay. Her polished guns were gleaming in the sun. Her rigging and billowed sails were singing. Soon, not far from the mangroves of the bay, Captain Carl ordered the ship at anchor. He summons his first mate,

"Skully ... pick two mates. We will set ashore and bury the chests."

Captain Carl leans over and whispers to Skully:

"Make sure they don't come back."

"Two scum it shall be, Captain." Skully calls out. "Snappy and Lump stand tall."

The crew lowers the longboat and the three large chests, two shovels, rope, and the four pirates: Captain Carl, Skully, Snappy, and Lump descend the rope ladder into the boat. Rowing through the smooth seas they soon disappear into the secret mangrove opening and into the mouth of Lake Surprise.

"There, there, by that large stump, set ashore." barks Captain Carl.

The boat slides softly into the wet sand. Captain Carl walks into the brush and selects a good spot to dig in the chests.

"Be lively, Mates. Dig deep."

Snappy and Lump dig well below the wet sand. The four lower the chests. Snappy and Lump cover the chests then turn only to be shot in the chest by Skully. Skully drags the two bodies into the bush. He sits them back to back, holding each other up, to rot in the sun.

"Two lazy bags of dirt they be," said Skully.

Captain Carl and Skully row out into the lake and back through the mangrove opening into the bay. They are shocked to see their ship is nowhere in sight, long gone into the horizon. *Little did Captain Carl and Skully know, the crew had emptied the chests and filled them with rocks.*

"Those dogs, those scurvy dogs. We'll find them. My blade will pass through each one of them after they rot in the sun roped to the gunnels near death," said the Captain."

"Filthy scum they be, Captain. My sword will follow yours," said Skully.

"Row along the shore of the bay Skully until we find a suitable mooring. We don't need them. We will live like Kings."

Two hours later they pull ashore at an old dock jutting out into the bay. Looking into the evening mist there appears to be a small settlement.

'Skully ... tender the boat to the dock and we'll knock back rum aplenty."

Skully climbs out of the boat, ties it to the dock, then turns to assist the Captain out of the boat. Just then, Skully, blinded by the setting sun, is shot by the Captain in the forehead and reels back until he runs out of dock and falls backward into the bay, soon to disappear into the murky water.

A few hours later, the Captain has arranged a bed for the night and is slumped over a large mug of spiced rum and a plate of baked fish at the Rusty Blade. He relishes in his position. He will retire with plenty of treasure. He sees himself laughing and rolling on the ground covered in gold. The next morning, fully refreshed, he sets off back to the treasure to get some of the money to fund his island paradise retirement.

As he rows out, full of excitement, he begins to struggle with the currents. He fights to hold his line down the shore, but is soon being drawn out to sea. In agony, he surveys his situation. Later that day he looks back and cannot see land at all in any direction. The next morning, the sun's heat on his face wakes him up. He desperately looks out and again, no sight of land. He is becoming very thirsty and begins to suffer delusions. He spends the day roasting in the sun.

The next morning he awakens to the sound of his crew clambering in celebration. He looks up and his ship is very near to him and a rope ladder is being lowered to receive him. Soon the ship is right beside his boat. He is filled with joy as he steps on the gunnel of the boat and steps forward to grab the ladder.

The Captain finds himself in the rolling seas. His illusion had sealed his fate. He struggles to reach back to the boat but the wind is moving the boat away from him. Frantically, he struggles to stay afloat. Thrashing in the sea, he is stung repeatedly in the face and hands by a swarm of sea nettle. He becomes partially paralyzed by venom. The Captain calls out:

"Lost ... all lost!"

The boat is left ... gently bobbing and moving toward the sunset.

MISSION X4123

A very boring situation is bearable if you have a good book.

THE YEAR IS 4123. PLANET EARTH IS A LIFELESS WASTE-land. The atmosphere is poisoned by an imbalance of various gases. The radiation levels will not support human life for perhaps thousands of years. The few humans who managed to escape the planet before it's demise in the year 2243, now reside on Zevelon, a small planet discovered in 2107.

Humans on Zevelon have developed a promising new mining process and proposed missions to Earth to exploit known rich silver deposits approximately eight miles west of where the city of Reno, Nevada was thought to have originally been located.

The second mission to planet Earth was conducted September 23, 2923. This mission established a landing pad with a Personnel Containment Lab (PCL). This facility provides shelter and comfort for mission personnel assigned to study of the current envoirnmental conditions on Earth. During the construction of the PCL, huge sections of steel, three feet thick were required to shield the workers from radiation. For the mining project to be

124

successful, the radiation levels must be within acceptable levels.

Since the initial mission in 2623, there have been four missions, 2923, 3223, and 3523, 3823 at three hundred year intervals as specified in the Master Protocol. It is forecasted that three additional missions may be required until the background radiation will allow human presence without shielding.

Captain Jack Wills reviews the summary document from the previous mission in 3823:

EXECUTIVE SUMMARY: Mission X3823
REPORT #X3823-Report-0089, Revision 1.

Mission crew conducted radiation data collection on June 06, 3723. This collection satisfies the three hundred year cycle of collection as specified in Protocol #X3823-PROC-00002, Revision F. The median data sample was 356 rem. This radiation level is less than the initial reading of 623 rem, in 2523. However, this reading is well above levels required to allow the mission crew to take readings outside of the existing PCL. Therefore, external exploration and mining is prohibitive. The next scheduled mission to Earth is in 4123.

Captain Wills reads the Master Protocol #X4123-PROC-00002, Revision D. He briefs his staff and crew and soon the 4123 mission is underway.

"Lieutenant Charles, perform all deployment equipment checks. We should be picking up the Earth's gravity field in about one hour," ordered the Captain.

"Aye, Aye, Skipper."

"Zevelon 6, this is Captain Jack Wills, Mission X4123-04, Mission Commander."

"Go ahead, Captain Wills."

"Base, we are one hour out from the Earth's gravitational field. Entry and PCL interlock equipment checks are in progress."

"Check, Protocols checked off. Advise at vehicle descent and PCL Interlock."

"All hands, this is the Captain. We are proceeding with all equipment checks and estimated entry into the Earth's atmosphere is in approximately one hour. All hands will be suited for entry and strapped for descent by 0413. Those assigned to secure the landing vehicle to the PCL, proceed with checks and verifications."

One hour and seven minutes later:

"Zevelron 6, this is Captain Jack Wills, Mission X4123-04, Mission Commander. We have landed on the PCL Pad and are stable. Checks are under way for PCL Interlock."

The crew determines that the exterior PCL monitor reads 178 rem. They complete the interlock to the PCL, and perform environmental checks of the PCL interior. The mission crew, Captain Wills, Lieutenant Charles, and Crewman Lacy and Compton enter the PCL.

"OK, let's settle in. Pick a bunk. It's home for the next five days," said the Captain.

"This place stinks! Captain, we need to check the air purification system," said Lacy.

"Funny how things change in three hundred years," said Compton.

"Captain, I don't know how past teams have managed to stay in such cramped quarters for weeks at a time. I'm ready when you are to get the hell out of here," said Lacy.

"Yeh ..." said the Captain. "Maybe six hundred years ago when they designed this paradise people could handle this place."

Over the following days, the various data points are monitored for radiation levels remotely from the PCL. The radiation levels remain unacceptable, but all data points are logged. By the forth day, nerves are wearing thin. The boredom is unbearable.

Lieutenant Charles looks out over the landscape. There is no life whatsoever. The soil is yellowish. Rocks outcrop. There is a blue-green liquid oozing from the soil.

"Damn, I'm going crazy in this PCL! What's up with Lacy? He's been very quiet. Every time I see him he has his face stuffed in a book. I didn't know we had any books in this paradise," said Skip Compton.

"No, we don't. They stopped making those things hundreds of years ago," said Wills.

"Yeh … this whole PCL thing gives me the creeps. This thing is nothing like the simulator. I feel like I'm inside a see-through golf ball," said Lacy.

"Look, we've got two more sets of readings to take. Let's all just settle down," said the Captain.

"At least back on Zevelon there's some things to look at. Those criminals from Zyron totally destroyed this planet," said Compton. "Hey, Lacy, what's up with that book? I didn't know any of those even existed any more."

"Well, when I put my stuff into the bunk drawer, I found this old book that someone from a previous crew must have left. It's difficult to read because it's falling apart."

"It must be some kind of book," said Compton. "You have had that thing to your face since we got here. What's the book about?"

"It's a collection of quirky short stories. The book is called *Tales from Prickly Path*. The prologue says the stories will give you a roller coaster of emotions. Does anyone know what 'roller coaster' means?"

Three TV's

Three fun TV stories.

TV #1:

I can't remember exactly when I bought my first new TV. All I remember was it was a very exciting day. In college, I had an old beat up used 12 inch dingy white TV. You will find how it met it's demise in the story: TV #3.

Anyway, with much anticipation, I entered the appliance section of large retail store to buy my first brand new TV. Even back then, there were many, many, TV's, all tuned to the same station. It took a while to work through all the various brands and sizes, but I finally settled on a set.

I motioned to a salesman and he came over all bright-eyed:

"Yes, sir. It's a fine day to buy a TV." he stated.

"Thanks! I've picked out this 16 inch that's marked down. Can you tell me about this TV and why it's marked down?"

"Sure," said the salesman. "This set is a dandy. It comes with auto focus. In addition, get this: if your remote is misplaced, you just say *remote* loud enough, and it starts beeping. It's last year's model. You could step up to a newer set, but it's quite a bit more, with basically the same features. We had a roof leak a few months ago and the boxes of the remaining sets got wet. The TV's are fine though."

"Well, I guess I'll take one," I said.

"I can't give you the floor model, so I'll go back in storage and pull one out for you."

Several minutes later the salesman came back out of the storage room, struggling, and holding his arms around the box. Just as he was about to set it on the counter by the register, the TV fell through the bottom of the box and crashed onto the floor.

"Well ... I guess if you want this one, I'll give you a really big discount."

TV #2:

Back in the mid-seventies my buddies and I were looking for furniture for an apartment we had recently rented. We saw an ad in the paper for three rooms of furniture, including a TV with stand, all for $499.00. We decided to go down to the furniture store to check it out.

A salesman that looked like he needed a drink and slept in his clothes the previous night, greeted us:

"Good afternoon, gentlemen! May I interest you in some fine furniture?"

"Well, we're here to see the three rooms of furniture for $499.00."

The salesmen moved closer to us, looked in either direction, and said:

"Look, I just work here, but you really don't want that promotional junk. That's just to get you into the store. For a few bucks more I can get you guys some quality furniture."

"Just how *"few"* bucks are you talking?"

"About $200.00."

"Well, we'd like to see the advertised grouping anyway."

"OK, follow me."

We turned the corner and there it was. I've seen cheap stick furniture but this was more like twig furniture. The material on the couch looked like it was made from some old drapes. The end table was missing a leg. The bed frames were all rusted. The TV looked like it was twenty years old. The salesman could tell we were disgusted.

"Well, I told you guys."

"Does the TV work? I asked.

"No, I think it just needs a new tube. Is it important to have a TV?"

"Why, yes, we need a TV."

"Look ... let me show you what you can get for just $200.00 more."

We were taken to another area of the store to see the $699.00 grouping. It looked just like the advertised grouping, except it was dusted off. The end table had all four legs and there was no TV.

"You see what I mean guys ... now, *this* is quality."

We looked at each other, turned, and started making our way to the front door.

"Gentlemen, gentleman ... you look like nice guys. Since it's the end of the month, I'm going to give you a great deal, today only, on this grouping. I'm going to take off $20.00 from the $699.00 for this grouping ... and I'm even going to throw in that old TV that doesn't work."

TV #3:
Remember the old 12 inch TV eluded to in the TV #1 story? I had owned that TV for years. It actually worked OK if all the tin foil on the antenna was adjusted just right. A thousandth of an inch movement would often mean

the difference between no picture, a snowy picture, or a blizzard.

Over time I got disgusted with always fiddling with the antenna ears and tin foil balls. I decided to investigate a rooftop mounted antenna. I went upstairs on the rooftop to investigate where I could mount the antenna. Then, it occurred to me: rather than buy an expensive antenna, I could just wire into an existing antenna. I went down to Radio Shack and bought 100 feet of antenna wire.

I went back up to the roof and connected the two antenna leads to an existing antenna. Then I lined up the wire even with my window, three floors below, and dropped the wire. I went back down to my apartment, opened the window, and used a broom to fish in the wire.

I pitched the old "rabbit ears" antenna with the foil balls. I coiled up the extra wire, then attached the two leads to the back of my TV.

The big game started in seven minutes. I had little time to spare. I slapped together a ham and cheese sandwich, grabbed a bottle of suds and sunk into my TV chair.

I turned on the set and was pleased to find that I had far less snow and I actually got a few extra channels. I tuned into the game. Just then, I noticed out the window that the cable was jiggling. Then, all of a sudden, the coil of cable on the floor was reeling out. The TV rotated to the left, flew off the stand onto the floor, slid across the floor, lifted up the wall and became lodged under the window ledge. Suddenly the wires snapped off the terminals and the TV crashed to the floor. The cable disappeared from view, never to be seen again.

* * *

That was the end of my old white, 12 inch TV. You might have thought that I would be disgusted. I was, but what really got me was when I got up to put mustard on my sandwich and found the jar was empty.

Oh No, Not Again

A very valuable coincidence.

BILL LUTZ IS WALKING DOWN MARKET STREET IN WILM-ington, North Carolina. He had recently ridden a bus into town. He is down on his luck. The hot sun seems to be melting the bottom of his shoes. Still he keeps walking, hoping the next step will bring something better than the last. As he stops to languish over his situation, his cell phone rings:

"Is this Mr. William Lutz?"

"Why, yes, it is. Who is this?"

"Mr. Lutz, this is Frederick Jones from Richter's Appliances, in Raleigh. Do you remember purchasing a used VRC from us three months ago?"

"Yes, I do believe I remember. I sold it. "

"Well, Mr. Lutz, when you bought that VCR you filled out an entry card to win a 50" color TV and you are our winner. When can you come to pick it up?"

Several blocks way, Tootie Revell is busy in his garden. He moved to Wilmington from Franklin, MA three years ago. He looked for months to find just the right place to call home. He gave up on living by the water because of the cost, but found a house with a big front porch. Across the street were deep woods that afforded him some privacy. He enjoyed sitting out on the porch looking deep into the woods and daydreaming.

Later that day, Tootie went out on errands. He just had come out of the drug store, started the car, and lowered his front door windows to let the heat escape. All of a sudden he felt cold steel against the side of his neck.

"Get out of the car, idiot, and leave the keys in the ignition."

Tootie complies. Bill Lutz hops in the front seat and is soon out of sight. Tootie calls the police to report the theft.

Bill is soon out of town headed for Raleigh. He plans on claiming the TV then pawning it for maybe as much as eight hundred dollars. He might be able to sell the car also. Several hours later he makes it to the appliance shop.

"Is Mr. Jones here?"

"Yes, I'm Frederick Jones."

"Great, Frederick, I'm Bill Lutz. I'm here to claim my TV."

"Sure, Mr. Lutz. Do you mind if we get a picture of you accepting the prize? "

"No, that's fine. But I really need to be going."

They take a few pictures of him standing next to the TV and an assistant helps Bill load the TV into his car. The only place it will fit is the back seat. Bill decides to leave North Carolina, maybe for Florida. He stops at a department store to get a bed sheet to cover the TV.

Meanwhile, in a small apartment across the street from the department store, a drug gang is meeting:

"Lenny, the police are looking for me and my car. You'll need to steal a car and take this money to Sticks in Hackensack. Don't skim anything out of the bag either. There's exactly forty grand in there and it better all make it to Sticks. He'll take care of you on the other end. Call me when you've made the drop."

A short while later, Bill walks up to the car and covers the TV with the sheet. He decides to check out the trunk to see if anything is in it. Just as he opens it, he feels something sharp in his side.

"Give me the keys to this car and you won't get hurt. Let's go."

Lenny stuffs the small suitcase full of money behind the driver's seat and is soon on the road headed for New Jersey. After a few hours he stops off in a rest area to go to the bathroom and get a cup of coffee. When he gets back to the car he opens the back driver side door to check on the money and see what's under the sheet. Just then, a young man and his girlfriend confront him. They have a handgun.

"Sorry, Mister, my girl and I need a ride down south and you just volunteered this car."

"Oh, no, not again. You can't take this car. I just stole it myself."

"I don't care if the Pope stole it. Right now, it's ours. Let's see those keys." growled the young man.

"At least let me get my bag out of the car," said Lenny.

"Sorry, get lost buddy before you make me use this. The last time I had this in my hand I shot a guy in the chest and I kind of liked it."

"Look. I really need that bag. All my family pictures are in that bag."

The man grabs the keys from Lenny.

Lenny figures he's toast if he loses the money so he leaps toward the man to try to get the gun. He is shot in the chest.

"Damn that felt good. Let's ride baby."

The young man and his girlfriend get into the car and take off headed back south. They decide to stay off Route 95, favoring Route 1 along the coast. As the man is driving, the girl turns to look under the sheet.

"Jimmy, Jimmy, it's a giant TV, brand new"

Neither notice the gym bag in the well behind the seat. They stop for gas and buy a week's worth of groceries in Wilmington. As they are relaxing eating an ice cream cone, Jimmy notices two policeman pointing toward the car. They take off and the chase is on. The couple manages to lose the police briefly in a residential area and decide they must ditch the car and make a run for it. They turn a corner, spot some woods, pull up and slam on the brakes. They fling the doors open, throw the keys, and make a desperate dash for the cover of the deep woods.

Tootie is washing dishes and glances out his window. He can't believe his eyes. A car, not far down the street, looks just like his. He rushes out there and finds the keys on the ground.

He looks under the sheet and finds the TV. Below the TV, in the well behind the driver's seat, he also notices the gym bag. He lifts it out and opens it. His eyes pop out of the sockets as he peels through the stacks of twenty dollar bills. Then he opens the trunk and finds six bags of groceries. He starts the car up to move it right across from his house and sees that he also has a full tank of gas.

He thinks to himself, Wow, maybe I'll be lucky enough and get my car stolen again some day!

Otis and Wally

A story of friendship.

SUNNYVALE ASSISTED LIVING CENTER IN SANTA MONICA, California, is only about a mile from the ocean, but for those who call Sunnyvale home, it might as well be a thousand miles. The center operates with a small city subsidy and private donations. Many of its residents led difficult lives in the city and never saw the ocean.

Otis Campbell moved into Sunnyvale when he was in his fifties. Early in his life he had alcohol problems and difficulty holding a job. The little family he had basically disowned him. One late morning the staff found him passed out on the front steps grasping a bottle wrapped in a paper bag. Fortunately, as the years rolled by, Otis enjoyed a sober life.

Wally Daniels worked hard throughout his life, but later in life he lost his eyesight to diabetes. He had no local family and his only option was to ask for assistance from the state. He was very happy to live at Sunnyvale.

When Otis and Wally met they became fast friends. Their rooms were just down the hall from one another, and they spent much of the day together. They played checkers in the morning and bingo in the afternoon. Otis

137

played his and Wally's bingo card. Wally was there for moral support. The two talked often of life. They shared many stories. One day while sitting out on the front porch, they asked each other what they wished they could have done in life:

"I wish I had gone to see the pyramids in Egypt. What's yours, Wally?" said Otis.

"Well, mine is nothing like yours. I know I can't see the ocean, but I've always wanted to walk the beach, smell the salt air, and feel and hear the ocean. I've only seen the ocean on TV years ago before I became blind."

"Really, Wally, that's such a simple thing. I was there once, I think, but I was drunk," said Otis.

"Not for me," said Wally. "I'm blind. There are many things I have not experienced."

Several years ago, there was talk here at the center about a group trip to the beach. It was squashed because of liability concerns and lack of staff.

"Wally, I know this sounds crazy but maybe we could sneak out of here and go to the ocean."

"What! Otis there's no way we could get out of here. They watch us all the time. This place is like Fort Knox. No one has ever just walked out of this place. There's always someone at the front desk."

"Maybe, but we're Wally and Otis and we can do anything. Wally, we can do this, but we need to come up with a plan."

Over the next few days Otis and Wally conspire. Otis read that the moon would be full in a few days. They will need their buddy, Wilber, to help out. There's only one problem, Wilber, 87, has a very bad memory.

Otis and Wally talk with Wilber and hatch a plan. Otis will place a large empty box in the downstairs hall closet. Otis and Wally will hide behind the couch in the lobby.

Wilber will come down to the lobby and ask the person at the desk to help him lift the bulky box to his room, just around the corner. With the desk person distracted, Otis and Wally will make a break for the front door.

The big day arrives. Otis stuffs his and Wally's bed and pulls up the covers to make it look like they are in bed. At exactly 7p.m., they work their way down the hall and hide behind the big couch in the lobby. Right on time, Wilber walks up to the front desk. He becomes confused and forgets what he was there to do.

Fortunately, the lady at the desk senses his confusion, gets up and begins to walk him back down the hallway to his room. Otis grabs Wally's hand and they spring for the front door, rocket through, and quietly close the door behind them.

Down the steps and down the street they are overwhelmed with joy and laughing uncontrollably.

"I can't see a thing, but I feel so free! Free!" said Wally.

"My God, we did it, Wally. We did it," said Otis. "Let's get going, we only have a few hours before it gets dark."

With a spring in their step, they head toward the setting sun. Where the sun sets, so shall Wally walk the beach for the first time. They make it several blocks, then trouble. Some punks note Wally is blind and pounce on the opportunity. They force Otis and Wally over into a nearby alley.

"Give us your money, you old fools."

"We don't have any money," said Otis.

The punks start pushing them around. Wally is terrified and just then he is slapped.

Otis cries out, "Let him alone! He is blind and I told you we have no money."

The thugs reach into Otis and Wally's pockets and find nothing except a small wooden cross that Otis had carved years ago. The thug throws it carelessly to the pavement.

139

Otis leans over to pick it up and is kneed in the stomach. The thugs laugh and walk off, disappearing into the cityscape.

The two embrace and leave the alley. Soon they are within view of the ocean. The sun is low in the sky.

"Wally ... I see the ocean. I see the ocean," said an excited Otis.

"My, God, thank you. Thank you," said Wally.

Just then, "Stop, you two." Wally and Otis turn to face a police officer. The officer is concerned because he knows the two are elderly and darkness is falling.

"Where are you two going?"

"Ah ... we're going to walk the beach."

"May I see your identification?"

"Ah ... we don't have any officer."

"Where do you live?"

"We live at the Sunnyvale Assisted Living Center."

"OK ... Let's get you back there. My squad car is just down the street."

"Officer, I promised my friend, Wally, who has never seen the ocean, that I would take him there. It's really important. It's the only life wish in his Bucket."

The officer notices that Otis is fumbling a small cross between his hands. Wally has tears in his eyes and is facing into the salty breeze.

"Ok, I'll run you guys down there for a few minutes, then I'm taking you back."

The officer pulls up close to where the surf is rolling in. Otis and Wally jump out.

"Otis, Otis ... I smell the sea ... it's wonderful! I hear the waves coming ashore. I never would have realized how wonderful and powerful this is!"

"Let's kick our shoes off. Take my hand, Wally. Let's run into the surf."

Wally takes his hand and they race off into the foaming surf.

As Wally runs across the wet sand the surf rolls over his feet. The aroma of the sea and sound of the rolling waves overwhelms him with joy.

"Wally, I'm so happy I was able to get you here. To me, it's just as good as seeing the Pyramids. We should be so thankful that we made it here."

"Yes, Otis, I am most thankful, but I am even more thankful to have you as my friend."

Of course, when they returned to the center they got chewed out. The next day, hunched over a steaming bowl of broccoli soup, they laughed and laughed.

Premonition

A story based on the customs of the Wampanoag Indians.

LONG BEFORE THERE WAS THE FAMED JETHRO COFFIN HOUSE, *or any English presence on Nantucket Island, there was an Indian tribe, the Wampanoag's (People of the Dawn). They lived peacefully on the beautiful island and thrived during all seasons. The ocean and inland ponds brought forth fish in abundance. The rolling hillside brought forth wildlife, berries, and nuts. They cultivated the land and lived on corn, beans, and squash. According to their lore, the islands that became Martha's Vineyard and Nantucket, were formed by a giant named "Maushop," who emptied his large moccasins full of sand into the ocean to form the islands.*

In 1998, two graduate Anthropology students were digging in sand dunes on Siasconset Beach. They were in search of artifacts from early settlement on the Island. Digging deep, Phil finds an old broken up tree stump and what appears to be the partial remains of an animal pelt.

"Hey, Vince ... check this out"

Phil holds up the small, fragile skin fragment to show Vince. Vince looks at it and says:

"Pretty cool ... that small hole in the skin looks like it could have been from a bullet or maybe an arrow."

"Yeh ... Let's keep looking. Maybe we can find something interesting."

* * *

In 1637 the Wampanoag's had the island to themselves. There were four tribes on the island, in different areas, that got along peacefully. It never occurred to them that soon they would have to share and eventually lose the island.

None of that mattered to Wamsutta. As a young boy, he ran over the sand dunes and through the woods, playing with other kids. He loved chasing butterflies and sometimes would chase them for miles.

As he got older he was very attracted to one of his childhood playmates, Askamaboo. They started spending a lot of time together and the families noticed. One day while the tribe was cleaning a "Pootop", or beached whale, the two lovers worked side-by-side giggling and carrying on all day. The families approved of their love.

One night Metacom, Askamaboo's father, awoke screaming from a nightmare.

"Are you alright, Father?" said Askamaboo.

"Yes, dear, I'll be fine," said Metacom.

One day, when Metacom was returning from a hunt, Wamsutta asked to speak to him in private. Wamsutta respected Metacom. Metacom was an important tribal elder and was endeared by all.

"Metacom, I am asking your permission to marry your daughter."

Metacom was not going to give away Askamaboo until Wamsutta proved his manhood and love for his daughter.

"Wamsutta, you like to run and chase. Your chase has led you to Askamaboo. Now, I ask you to chase down a deer and bring that deer to me alive."

Wamsutta had often chased raccoons, skunks, and other animals, but had never chased a deer. He gave up on rabbits. He thought to himself it would be very difficult to chase a deer.

"I love Askamaboo dearly. I will start my chase tomorrow at dusk. I will gather provisions."

"Wamsutta, you will not be chasing just any deer. You will be chasing a deer with an arrow in its neck. The arrow has been in the deer's neck for many moons."

"Yes, Metacom, I have seen that deer grazing on occasion. I will find it, chase it down, and bring it back to you. It is an honor for me to do this for you and an honor to be considered for the hand of your daughter."

Wamsutta knows he needs lots of rest during the day, for deer are active at night and rest during the day. He knows he will only be able to chase the deer at night since their hiding places are very hard to find during the day. The only way to catch the deer is to chase it relentlessly until it is so tired it cannot run any further. That means he must be more determined than the deer. He hopes to bring back the deer in no more than a few days.

At dusk the following day, Wamsutta and Askamaboo embrace and Wamsutta says goodbye to the families and sets out. Early on he sees many deer, but after five days of searching on the island there is no sight of the deer with an arrow in its neck. He wonders whether the deer may have perished or had been taken by another tribe member from a different part of the island.

Finally, early on the sixth day, just beyond a large dune, he finds the deer, along with others, resting in the tall grass. He is dog-tired, but decides later that day to try to work the deer onto the wet sand. He feels if he chases the deer in the wet sand, the deer will tire.

That night, he begins tracking the dear. He follows, down wind, from afar. Suddenly, in the moonlight, there they are, grazing adjacent to the dunes. He must separate his deer from the herd, and continue his chase plan.

He readies himself for the chase. He tightens up his backpack and takes off after the deer. The deer is much faster, but he keeps it in sight and continues maneuvering it toward the ocean. He is gaining on the deer. On the eighth day, he just cannot keep up. He falls exhausted. Late in the day, he is surprised to find the deer, along with other deer, are grazing very close to where he is resting. He chases the deer most of the night toward the surf. Running like the wind, both struggling in the wet sand, the deer stumbles and falls, frightened and exhausted. Wamsutta falls beside his prize. He is gasping for air. The deer is too exhausted to rise. He places the harness he had packed around the deer's neck and ties the line around his waist. There, in the foaming surf, they both slept, exhausted.

Three days later, Wamsutta enters the camp with the prized deer. Instead of being cheerfully greeted by the tribe he finds a somber atmosphere. Askamaboo runs up, embraces him, then begins crying.

Metacom had died two days earlier. Wamsutta finds the tribe is preparing for his burial. A deep hole is prepared for his body. According to custom, the family members paint their faces with black soot and gather to morn the Indian leader. He is then lowered into the sand, with the tools required to cultivate his crops in the land beyond placed by his side. The mat he was lying on when he died is placed over him, and the bowl in which he had his last meal was then placed on the mat. The burial plot was entirely covered and mounded with sand. The final remembrance, according to Wampanoag burial custom, is to hang a fine animal skin from a nearby tree.

Singing Birds

A bitter snowstorm, but the birds will always sing.

ANYONE WILL TELL YOU: WINTER IN THE EDMORE, NORTH Dakota is always memorable. I guess some winters are more memorable than others. The winter of 1949 was one of the most memorable. Early in March, the dark gray skies, with even darker clouds, were swirling over the Clausen's old farmhouse on their sixty acres. Sam and Clara had farmed the land for years, but now just lease the land out and take things real easy like. As easy like as you can in Edmore.

Day 1, March 8, 1949
There was an icy silence in the Clausen's home. Even though Sam and Clara had seen a lifetime of snowstorms in Edmore, something was different this time and they both felt it. The local news talked about a heavy snowstorm that could linger if the cold front stalled due to high pressure from the east. The storm was to hit late that night.

They have always been well prepared for these storms. They were lucky for this one for they were retired and could just ride it out, just like they always had in previous years.

"Well, Sam. Here we go again," said Clara.

"Yeh ... I'll start bringing in extra firewood. Ya know, Clara, these really bad storms come every five years or so. Maybe, this one will be our last."

Clara laughed, "Maybe. Let's get through our forty-third anniversary on the fourteenth first."

Day 2, March 9, 1949

Clara is at the living room window sitting in her favorite chair watching the large snow flakes gently piling up on top of each other. She thinks back to when she was growing up in Edmore and how she used to bundle up in a snow suit and play outside for hours. She hated to have to come in when supper was called.

"Sam, come look at the beautiful, large snowflakes."

"Wow," said Sam. "Those are big flakes. They are the kind that really pile up."

Clara gets up, walks over to the window and says, "The weatherman said we may get a foot today. With the four inches from last night, that's close to a foot and a half."

"What's for supper tonight, Clara?"

"I'm making your favorite, beef stew."

Day 3, March 10, 1949

It takes Sam forever to bundle up for the long walk, close to a quarter-mile down the driveway to get to the mailbox. He would usually ride down in his truck, but the snow is too deep. He decides to walk. Once back, he brings in five armloads of wood for the fireplace.

Clara is busy in the kitchen. The corn bread is almost done. She says to herself, "I hope this all clears up before our wedding anniversary on the fourteenth." She thinks of Spring. Sam had mentioned that he wished he had a tape recorder to record all the beautiful bird sounds. Clara had recently bought Sam a small tape recorder to give to him as an anniversary gift. She got the battery version so Sam could use it anywhere. She was excited. She had recorded a message for him and set it to play at 5p.m. on the fourteenth. The gift is hidden in the kitchen drawer and would begin to play just as they were having supper on that special night.

"I smell cornbread!" says Sam as he enters the back part of the house where the kitchen is.

"It's nice and wet, Sam. I know how you like your cornbread. It's still snowing. I don't believe there's been a break. The news just started. Lets see what they say about this snow." Sam turns on the set:

"Folks in Northeast North Dakota need to honker down. The current storm is a doozy even by North Dakota standards. It's -8 degrees right now. The low for the night may reach as low as -15. The cold front is stalled over north central North Dakota. An emergency number, 767-675-8976, has been established."

"You won't hear any birds singing today I'll tell you," said Sam. They're smart. In the winter they get the hell out of here."

"Do you think there are beautiful singing birds in Heaven, Sam?"

"There must be," said Sam. "I can't imagine Heaven without birds."

Day 4, March 11, 1949

It's late afternoon. Sam and Clara are sitting in the kitchen having coffee, looking out at the snow, listening to the radio, when they hear a loud snap and the power goes out. Heavy ice had accumulated on the power line and it let go.

Like well-oiled machines, Clara and Sam spring into action: Clara gathers, distributes, and lights the candles. Sam adds logs to the fire. They have been without power before and they are ready. They would call the utility, but like in the past are told that they will be out when they can, no time soon. Besides, the phone was out, also. Sam closes various doors in the house to conserve the heat from the fireplace.

"We'll bundle up for sure tonight, Clara."

"What's for supper tonight, Clara?"

"Your second favorite, leftover beef stew, wood fired, served with cornbread."

Day 5, March 12, 1949

The house is cold in the morning, but soon Clara is busy cooking breakfast over the fireplace.

They spend a lazy day together sipping coffee and talking about all the places they have been, friends and family, and silly things. The silly things that endear.

That night they sit beside each other on the couch in the dark and watch the moonlit display of a snowy wonderland.

Day 6, March 13, 1949

Clara is up early and busy making an apple pie. It's Sam's favorite dessert and she wants it all ready for the big day tomorrow. She looks out at the snowy fields.

Outside, Sam is loading up firewood. He lifts the last load onto a small sled and begins to drag it across the deep snow toward the house. Just then he suffers a debilitating heart attack. He cries out. A cry that only the bitter cold winds will hear.

Clara is busy in the house with bed making and such. She wonders why Sam is taking so long getting the firewood. She puts on a robe and opens the back door off the kitchen and steps out.

"Sam ... Sam ... Can you hear me?"

The bitter wind briefly forces her back inside. She goes back out and yells out again several times then decides to step further out and try to see him. As she does, the door behind her locks shut. She peers around the side of the house and does not see Sam. She calls out repeatedly and now is very worried. She walks out in the deep snow around the side of the house. Suddenly, she sees him slumped over the sled and rushes over. She lays him on his back in the snow and feverishly tries to revive him, but soon realizes that he has died. She lies down beside Sam and draws him in. She feels a sense of warmth and contentment and becomes very sleepy.

Day 7, March 14, 1949

There was an icy silence in the Clausen's home. At supper time, Clara's voice is heard from a closed drawer in the kitchen:

"My dear, Sam. Here is the tape recorder you always wanted and I dearly wanted you to have. You see, I love the sounds of the birds, also. I hope we will hear their sweet sounds together, always. Happy anniversary, my dear."

Outside, out of the gray skies, a single ray of sunlight shines on the couple embraced in the snow.

Texas Justice

Don't mess with Texas.

"OK, HANDS UP, UP HIGH. DON'T LOOK AT ME. LOOK AND you're a dead man."

Warren Spreads, alias Wally Upton, was out on bail again. This time, he said, as a changed man. Maybe, but to fool the police, he changed from robbing liquor stores to robbing convenience stores. He had a rap sheet that ran out the door, and around the corner, and up the stairs into the attic. His first arrest, after he was warned several times, was for stealing yo-yo's from the local dime store when he was only seven. As he grew, so did his reputation. He acquired zest for the criminal lifestyle.

His mother, Aggie Mae Spreads died shortly after his dad left her for a new life in Atlanta. No one had heard from him since. That left Warren's grandmother, Miss Ellie, to care for young Warren.

Warren was ruthless. He didn't just want to steal things, he wanted to be the best at it. He wanted people to notice. He wanted to be somebody big. Warren knew that another armed robbery arrest would mean his criminal days were over. That didn't phase him, robbery was in his blood, stream deep.

"Let's go! I don't have all night."

"Sir, please do not rob me. My family has so little money," pleaded Mohammed, the store owner. He cowered, but slowly reached under the counter and pushed the emergency button.

"Shut up, open that cash register and lie down on the floor with hands over your head. Did you hear me, camel jockey? Get those hands over your head ... now."

"Sir, please don't steal from me and my family."

"Shut up, shut up, don't say anything else or you won't see your family again.

As Warren starts to empty the register, a woman enters the store. Warren points his gun at her and shouts:

"Get over there by that ATM machine, lie down and keep you're mouth shut. Now! Don't look at me. Do you understand?"

The young woman complies, but looks intently out the window. Warren notices her looking and looks also. A first responder, a Texas Ranger, is approaching slowly, being careful to stay out of sight.

Warren yells, "Don't nobody move or say anything."

The Ranger peers into the store then enters. Warren jumps out from behind a display stand and shoots the Ranger fatally in the chest. He grabs the last of the cash and runs out of the store, disappearing into the darkness of the ghetto jungle.

Ranger Tim Buchanan, had been on the force only three years and leaves behind a wife and four children. Soon the crime scene is established. The witnesses give a good description of the robber to the police. They believe Warren Spreads is the killer. Soon the entire Police community is mobilized.

Miles away, in quiet Hobbs, Texas, Jesus Cravens, a local grain elevator worker leaves a small grocery store. He notices a tall blond loading her groceries into her trunk and decides to try to get to know her. A big blond like her really sticks out in Hobbs.

"Excuse me, miss. May I be of service loading your groceries?"

"No, thank you," the lady with a rough smoker's voice replied.

"Say. Are you from around here?" asked Jesus.

"No, just passing through. Have a good day."

Jesus looks closely at her. Something just doesn't seem right. He reaches out, grabs her hair and pulls her wig off.

"Ah ... just as I thought. Mister, we don't take kindly to *fruits* in this town."

"Who you calling a *fruit*?"

Fists start flying and the brawl catches the attention of a local town cop just finishing a meatball sandwich at Anne's, a local lunch favorite. The cop called for support and ran to break up the fight. Both men scuffle with the cop, and as more cops appeared, both men are subdued and arrested.

Soon after, Warren Spreads private life was at the end of the road. He was charged with Capital Murder along with a host of other charges. He was taken back to Lubbock, Texas, where he had robbed the convenience store. In three short months he was behind bars at the Men's Correctional Prison in Austin, Texas, while on appeal for his death sentence. Five months later it was decided to move Warren to the Men's Correctional Prison in Abilene, where the appeal was be heard.

The Texas Rangers were asked to escort the prisoner from the prison in Austin to the facility in Abilene. What should have been a routine prisoner escort, went horribly wrong, on a deserted stretch of highway, an hour out of Abilene.

According to the Rangers report, the escort, four cars in all, made a routine stop along the desolate highway to relieve themselves. The prisoner, in cuffs, decided to run for it and ran into an adjacent cornfield and was shot dead. Since the man's body appeared to have been heavily bruised in addition to bullet wounds, an autopsy was requested.

Several weeks later, following the autopsy results, a reporter for the Abilene Reporter asked the Commanding Ranger responsible for the escort for an interview.

"Major Creek. I'm sorry your prisoner escort ended badly."

"Yes, so am I, but these things happen when a prisoner makes a poor decision."

"Sir, the autopsy mentioned that the prisoner had several broken ribs and facial bones. Would you explain that?"

"Well, he did take a hard fall after being shot in the cornfield."

"The official report states that the prisoner ran about seventy-five feet into the cornfield when he was shot. Is this correct, sir?"

"Why, yes. I would say that's about right."

"Sir, the autopsy states that there were four .38 caliber bullet holes in the back of the prisoners head that would fit within the diameter of a silver dollar. The convict was shot about seventy-five feet into the cornfield. How do you explain this?"

"Well sir, my boys are real good shots."

That Exhilarating Feeling

Better keep your eye on the ball.

SAM COLLINS HAS ALWAYS WORKED HARD TO BE THE BEST. The best at everything. Generally, he would eventually emerge the best or close to it because he was a very patient hard worker. Once he put his mind to something he was tenacious.

When Sam took up golf, it was indeed his match. You are asking for trouble if you try to combine perfect and the game of golf. Like everything else, Sam immersed himself into the game. He works on all phases, driving, fairway shots, chip shots around the green, putting, and specialty shots. One day he hit sand shots from 4a.m. to darkness. Sam is spending more and more time at various golf courses convinced he may reach a zero handicap. He had finally found something that would severely test his patience.

"Sam!" said his wife, Molly, "look, what is going on here? You are becoming obsessed with this golf thing."

"I'm sorry, Molly. It is important to me. I want to play really well, not just OK. I want to feel that exhilarating feeling. It's not something silly like your flower arranging hobby."

"What!" How can you be so insensitive. Hasn't it occurred to you that I have important outlets and mine are every bit as important as yours?"

"Oh, come on Molly, really, flower arranging? Anyone can do that well. Look, I'm going out to play golf. I'll see you later."

Sam and Molly have had their spats in the past and most of the time it was over his quest to be the best at something. That night, Molly asks Sam to sit down and talk about their marriage. Sam is mad at himself because he had not played well that day.

"Sam, we need to talk about respect and your attention placed on our relationship."

"Oh no … not again. Now, what did I do?"

"Look Sam, over the years there's always been some obsession of yours that takes up all of your time. Time that we should be sharing together."

"We spend lots of time together."

"Yeh … like when?"

"Like when I took you to the company Christmas Party."

"Oh, come on, Sam. That's an event, not quality time. Let's go off for a weekend someplace exciting, maybe camping?"

"So, it's not exciting enough for you around here?"

Molly throws her dish towel on the counter and returns to the kitchen cleanup.

"I'll see you later. I'm going to hit some balls out."

"Why don't you try to get a hole in one?" said Molly. "That's supposed to be very difficult. That would really change your life won't it, to finally hit that perfect shot?"

Sam continues the next several weeks improving his game. He's convinced that by hitting lots of balls he can get a hole in one. If he can get a hole in one, he will be able to have a perfect achievement.

One night, when Sam was out playing golf, Molly decided to retire early. Before she went to bed, she sat at her dressing table. She looked longingly in the mirror. She kept tilting her face to lessen the shadows and wrinkles. She wondered where the years had gone and why her fairytale marriage never materialized. She turned to look at their marital bed and lowered her head. She could not look back into the mirror.

Several days passed.

"Well, Sam, have you got a hole in one yet? Look, you need a break. I got a brochure about a good camping spot up on Thomas Peak. Let's sit down and talk about it."

"No, Molly, no hole in one, but I'm working on it. Each day I get closer. My shots are falling mainly within ten feet or so. I just need to work a little more on my direction."

As the weeks roll by, Sam is getting closer. He's had lots of shots within ten inches from the cup.

"Sam, are you playing golf tomorrow?"

"Yes," answers Sam.

"About what time will you be back?"

"I should be back by 4p.m."

The very next day, Sam rushes out to the golf course. On the par three, 6th hole he lines up his seven iron and slices it right of the hole. The ball bounces off the cart path, careens toward the green, hits a water sprinkler head , rolls up onto the green, and ¼" off the lip of the cup. At the end of his round he rushes home all excited to tell Molly about how close he came to a hole in one.

As he comes flying through the door he finds the house completely empty except for a golf ball in the middle of the living room with a note under it. The note reads,

"I've gone in a different direction. I feel like I sank a hole in one. I've got that exhilarating feeling! Call Murray, if you are not too busy playing golf, he has some papers for you to sign."

The Ladies of the Mission

A story of two ladies who work tirelessly for the mission.

IF YOU LOOK ON THE WALL, OVER THE VEGETABLE TABLE IN the kitchen of the 136th Street Soup Kitchen Mission in Little Rock, Arkansas, you will find rough paintings of benefactors of the mission. Some contributed lots of money, some lots of time, but seldom both. Sweet Bobby Nichols, the long time salad man, painted several of the paintings, including Elsie McKane and Cynthia Parks Tipton. These two ladies were as different as different is. Yet, many commented on the strong resemblance between the two as depicted by Sweet Bobby. You see, Elsie was a woman of few means ... while Cynthia was a lady of privilege.

To the right of the painting of the old town judge is the painting of Cynthia Parks Tipton. She was sixty-three when she posed for the painting and looked as regal as the day she joined the Mission Board thirty-four years ago. Her father was a prominent Little Rock attorney. After her graduation from The University of Texas, Austin, she became a tireless fund raiser for the Mission, donating over a million dollars of her own money.

No one knew where Elsie McKane came from. One day, she just showed up at the kitchen with her shopping cart full of personal belongings and said she wanted to help out. That was years ago. She told people she was born during a thunderstorm in July of 1929. The rain pounded down so hard that the proud parents Bert and Clara could hardly hear each speak during their daughter's delivery. Little Elsie slept right through it all. Elsie had a smile that lit up the ramshackle Mission. She was there every day with a glow of the Lord's blessing. She would often say:

"Reach out, reach up, and behold the wonder of our Father. Peace live within us as an Empire."

She liked working the plate and utensil section of the line. She would straighten out everything.

"Neatness will prevail within the Lord's Table," she would often say. She worked the mornings and afternoons. When asked where she lived she replied:

"I live within the Lord's mansion."

When things slowed after breakfast, and again after lunch, Elsie took to the streets with her old shopping cart. She was drawn to the poor souls who lingered there in despair. Many of them could not make it to the Mission so she would bring food to them. Benny, a hopeless alcoholic, would slowly lift his head as she would approach. His glazed, watery eyes would blink and slowly focus on her. She would extend some food to him, and then lovingly stroke his forehead. Benny would look deep into Elsie's eyes, turn, and slowly extend his arms out, then raise them into the heavens.

"Reach out, reach up, and behold the wonder of our Father. Peace live within us as an Empire."

Elsie visited others, many others, endless misery, yet she brought an equal measure of hope. Somehow, no matter how many she fed, her shopping cart always had enough food to go around.

Cynthia Parks Tipton worked tirelessly to raise money for the mission. She held lavish fund raisers at her home. It was often said that she could get Jack Benny to give if she could get him to come to one of her events. Every year, in May, was the annual Mission Banquet. Local leaders, contributors, and honored guests gathered to support the Mission. Elsie McKane, honored for her work over the years, was often invited, but always declined:

"Too many fancy people for me."

Then one day, Cynthia Parks Tipton died of a sudden heart attack. Everyone at the mission was stunned and sad to lose her. About that same time, they noticed that Elsie was no where to be found. Some say she went back to where she had come from, wherever that was.

Shortly following Ms. Tipton's death, her secretary called the director of the Mission:

"Sir, this is Lilly Palmer, Ms. Tipton's secretary. Do you have a minute to talk?"

"Why, yes. I certainly do. We are so sorry to hear of her passing"

"Ms. Tipton's *Will and Testament* contains a rather large contribution to the mission. This donation will be electronically deposited like her other donations. In addition, she also wants to donate two personal items."

"Personal items?"

"Yes, a late model van, and oddly enough, an old shopping cart."

The Man from D Block

Sometimes miserable people may surprise you.

STUBBS MCAULEY HAS BEEN DOING TIME IN CELL 13, "D" Block at Alcatraz Prison for some forty-three years. He had been convicted of killing a cab driver in San Francisco and sentenced to life. He had come up for parole numerous times but was always passed over because of his miserable attitude and lack of remorse. At one hearing, he told the board the cab driver ... "had it coming and I hope he rots in Hell." Stubbs was a tough guy ... 1920's tough. He wore it like a medal on his chest.

William Mauldin was a young lawyer, fresh out of law school with a tender spot for the criminal mind. William attended law school with a Name Scholarship from a local university. The scholarship was for a student whose family name was "Mauldin." He was very fortunate because his mother had little money. Oddly enough, neither William nor his mother knew that his dad started the scholarship years ago.

William's mom, Mary, told her son years ago that his dad just left one day. Well, technically, that's right he *did* leave ... he left for prison. Over the years his dad sent many letters to his son but his mother intercepted and disposed

162

of the letters. She had no contact with her husband, never brought his name up and never visited him in prison. She did not want her son to know that his dad was a felon.

On a humid July night, William's mom passed away. Following her burial, William began going through her belongings and cleaning out her apartment.

While cleaning out under the sink, he reached under the sink and pulled out the small trash can and various cleaning supplies. He took his cleaning rag and was wiping under the sink when he noticed some debris stuffed in a back corner of the cabinet. He pulled the debris out, and amidst old ads and such, was a letter from seventeen years ago addressed to him.

As he read the letter he realized it was from his dad. The return address was Alcatraz Prison. One sentence of the letter said:

"Son, I don't know why you have never answered any of my letters or visited me. Maybe these letters are not getting to you."

* * *

William decided to visit his dad. He called the prison and found that the only man named Mauldin had died eight years ago. His body was taken by the city.

"Sir, would there be anyone there that knew my dad that I could talk to?"

"Yes, his best friend was Stubbs McAuley. He's a real tough guy. I can't let you talk to him on the phone, but you can visit him anytime. I doubt he will speak with you though. He has never had a visitor and is a dangerous, miserable individual. He is usually in solitary, "D" Block, but is in a holding cell at present."

William decides to try to visit Stubbs.

"McAuley, you have a visitor."

"A visitor. If it's a lawyer tell them to get lost."

"It's some guy by the name of William Mauldin."

"Mauldin! His name is Mauldin?... OK, I'll see him."

As Stubbs enters the visiting room William is taken aback by his presence. He is very rugged looking with a mean look.

"Are you a lawyer? If so, I don't have any money and I don't like lawyers."

"Why, yes, I am a lawyer. Did you know my father, Bill Mauldin?"

"Yeh, well it's none of your damn business," said Stubbs.

"Look, I'm here to learn about my father. He was incarcerated long before I was old enough to even get to know him. My mother never told me he was in jail. She just told me he walked out when I was very young. I understand you were friends with him."

"I don't have friends, kid. Your dad's name was Phillip, not Bill. He was a good man. He talked about you all the time. You helped him to cope with this place even though he never heard from you or saw you. He knew your worthless mother would cover everything up. Like a lot of people in this hole, he did something really stupid, and since he was a nobody he got screwed."

"My dad sent a letter, maybe many letters. I never saw them."

"Look, kid, I've got walls to stare at. Get lost."

*　*　*

William left and felt discouraged. He decided to research the background for the scholarship he was awarded to go to law school. To his surprise, it was started by his dad, Phillip Mauldin.

William went down to the college. He explained that he had found his father, and his father founded the "Mauldin" name scholarship. He asked the administrator to review the scholarship file. He was surprised to find that over a number of years his dad had contributed to the fund. Then, he noticed that his buddy, Stubbs McAuley had also made substantial deposits. Both men had sent in funds from their prison pay. Why would Stubbs contribute he thought?

The next day William went down to the city hall to see his dad's death certificate. His name was indeed Phillip, not Bill, as his mother had once told him. While he was there, he decided to view his own birth certificate. The certificate listed his mom and dad, Mary Simpson and Kenneth (Stubbs) McAuley.

The Road Trip

A father and son story made possible by a tragic event.

A SOFT VOICE MIXES WITH THE SMOKE, FLAMES, AND THE *freezing rain. "Awaken, awaken, Roger, Ritchie, J.P., and Buddy. Awaken all. Come very close to me. You will become whole and be at peace."*

"Billy, Billy, time to get up. This is the big day you have been waiting for."

"Ok Mom, thanks. I'll be right down."

Billy Miller, from Horton, Iowa, was an oldies music nut. Ever since he could reach up to turn on a radio he was hooked to music of the '50's. To him, the music of his day, the '80s just didn't have the same range of joy and pain. Mainly, his pain … the pain of a teenager.

From the minute he got up until he went to bed he listened to the oldies station. He saved money from his paper route to donate to the radio station.

His parents certainly understood why he loved the oldies and understood why he wanted to take a special road trip to see the monuments in the field as soon as he got his driver license. This was the day: Billy, with license in hand, and his dad, set out on the road trip.

"Dress warm. It's going to be cold up there out in that cornfield," said Billy's mom.

Billy was so excited. He would be driving the whole way, over and back, a total of about seven hours.

"Hey, Dad. I've got an idea. Let's pick our favorite oldies songs and explain why we like them."

"That's a great idea, Billy. Would you like me to go first?"

"Ok, Dad."

"Well, let's wait until we get on the back side of Charles City. That will give me some time to think about my five favorites."

Billy and his dad continue to drive toward Charles City.

"Not much to look at Billy unless you really like barren cornfields with snow patches. I'm ready to talk about my favorites. It's funny; they all tie into meeting and getting to know your mom."

"Great! Let's hear them, Dad."

"Well, my first favorite has to be "Let It Be Me." I met your Mom in high school. That was in 1960. We all came into the school as freshmen from different local middle schools. Those were very exciting and awkward times.

Billy, I fell in love with your mom the minute I laid eyes on her. She had a beautiful smile and was very graceful. We were in the same algebra class. She was smart. We talked some in class, but she didn't seem all that interested in me. All I remember is saying over and over: "Let It Be Me."

Throughout high school I would see her at different school functions. She was lovely. I would always make sure I was right there to talk with her. In our junior year she was going out with one of our star high jumpers from the track team, Applehead.

"Applehead? How did he get that name?"

"Well, his head was shaped like an apple. Anyway, I couldn't help but connect with songs like "My Prayer" by the Platters and "The Way You Look Tonight." I always kept the hope that your mom and I would be together.

My big break came in the fall of my senior year. I heard that your mom had broken up with Applehead. The Snowflake Ball was coming up near the end of November. I ran over to her house to ask her to be my date. It was the longest two or three seconds of my life … waiting for her answer, but she accepted. About that same time, Roy Orbison came out with "Running Scared." It was an instant favorite of mine, but in the back of my mind I was concerned that maybe Applehead would come back into the picture. He never did.

Your Mom and I became inseparable from then on. I remember one night lying in bed thinking what a lucky guy I was and another favorite, "At Last," by Etta James came on. Gosh, Billy, I still love your mom so much."

"Dad, that was powerful. I had no idea you and mom went through all of that. I guess I feel better now about myself. My feelings … now that I'm in high school. I have many favorite songs, but the song I think about all the time is "When I Fall in Love," by the Lettermen. Dad, I hope I meet someone nice and we build a future together like you and Mom did."

"I'm sure you will, Billy. All good things come in time."

Billy and his dad arrive in Clear Lake, Iowa, and walk out into a field located about three miles from the airport. Billy walks up to the monuments, reflects warmly for a few minutes, then bows his head and says a silent prayer. He turns to his dad and says:

"Thanks for coming on this trip with me, Dad. You know I have always wanted to come here. Sometimes I've thought I've been drawn here. But, this trip has been made special because I never thought that I would get to know so much about how you and Mom met and fell in love. It's wonderful that the music of that time played such a great part in your relationship with Mom. Dad, we will always share our mutual love of oldies together."

Twenty-four years earlier, February 4, 1959:

Good morning and welcome to the WKBK, Eyes On Iowa, early news. I'm Jimmy Peeler. I am sad to report an early morning fatal plane crash in Clear Lake. The small plane, piloted by Roger Peterson, went down in a field just after takeoff. Along with the pilot, national recording artists: J. P. (The Big Bopper) Richardson, Ritchie Valens, and Buddy Holly all perished.

They Were All There

A story about family and friends who celebrate our special events.

"DAD, DID YOU REMEMBER TO CALL AND SEE IF YOUR WATCH is ready to be picked up? I'm going by that way later today and I'd like to pick it up for you."

"No, son, I'm sorry. It escaped my mind. I'll call them in a few minutes."

"Well, with the big day coming up, I guess things would slip your mind. Gosh, ninety-five, what a milestone."

"Yes, it's an accomplishment, but I've told you many times, one hundred is my goal. My dad died at ninety-seven, and his dad, ninety-nine. I feel pretty good and I'm going for the big, one, zero, zero."

"That's the attitude, Dad. I'll call you later this afternoon."

Thomas Lynch is a retired engineer. He retired many years ago, but is quite active. Now his last goal in life is to sit in front of a big birthday cake on his one-hundredth birthday surrounded by all his family and friends.

Later that day, Thomas goes into the bathroom to freshen up. He looks intently into the cabinet mirror. Through his watery eyes he looks closely at the all the features of his rugged face and thinks about all the bumpy roads he has been down. Just then, his knees buckle slightly. He feels weak and supports himself on the sink. After a few minutes he returns to the living as the phone rings:

"Dad, did you remember to call and see if your watch is ready."

"No, Billy, I'm sorry."

"Well, I'm only a few blocks away, I'll just stop by the shop."

"I'm sorry, son, I don't know why I seem to be so forgetful."

"That's ok, Dad. See you at the big party on Tuesday."

Thomas hangs up the phone, slowly turns, and looks out the living room window. He sees a large tree that he does not recall ever seeing. He calls his son:

"Sonny Boy, I'm looking out the living room window next to the TV. There's a large tree out there that I don't recall."

"Dad, don't you remember? You and I planted that together. Remember, we had to keep it twenty-five feet away from the house because the tree would eventually have a wide root system? It's a very large tree."

"I'm sorry, I just don't remember. Well, we did a good job. That sure is a big healthy tree."

Tuesday arrives:
Thomas looks down at his refurbished watch that his son picked up for him. The doorbell rings and soon the house fills with family and friends. Kids are running through the house and it seems everyone is talking at the same time. Things settle down, cards and gifts are presented. The birthday candles are lit and the glow fills the small room. Thomas looks out at all the glowing faces. They were all there, some old, some young, some he thought he would

never see again, some he had not seen in years, and all gathered to honor him on this special day. A tear came to his eye as he wished that he would always remember this moment and he would see them all again in five years.

Several years later:
"Mr. Lynch, I'm sorry. Your father was admitted this morning to the emergency room here at Memorial Hospital. Please come here immediately and ask for Doctor Grassa."

Billy rushes down to the hospital and speaks with Doctor Grassa:

"Mr. Lynch. I'm sorry, but your dad has a very serious condition. He has a large tumor pushing against several large blood vessels to his heart. We are concerned about blood clots and outright blockage. We cannot operate because of his age. We have him on blood thinners. I'm sorry, your father may not live much longer ... a week or two at best. There's nothing more we can do for him, so we will move him to a room for a few days to monitor him until he is stable then he will be discharged."

Later that day, his dad is moved to a room in the hospital and Billy visits him:

"Hi, Dad. Hey ... what are you doing in here? You have stuff at the house you need to tend to."

His dad is very weak, but laughs and slightly lifts his head off the pillow and says in a low voice:

"Hi, Billy. The doctor spoke with me. I'm not sure what he said, but I know it's not good. I don't want to be sick and bedridden when my one-hundredth birthday comes along.

"What are you talking about, Dad? You just celebrated your one-hundredth."

"I did! I thought it was my ninety-fifth?

"No, Dad. You made it! You made it ... the big one, zero, zero!"

"I did it, I made it!" said Thomas.

Thomas returned home and quietly passed away during the night a month later. At the instant he died, Thomas opened his eyes. He felt a wonderful warmth. He looked out at all the glowing faces. They were all there, some old, some young, some he thought he would never see again, some he had not seen in years, and all gathered to honor him on this special day.

When Woody Met Meg

This one is dedicated to you, Woody.

EXCUSE ME, MISS. IS ANYONE SITTING HERE?" SAID WOODY.
"Why, no, please sit," said Meg.

Happy hour was packed at Wally's in East Aurora, New York, but Woody and Meg would soon find their own little corner of the universe.

"Whaddaya have, Buddy?" said the bartender with a disgusted look on his face.

"I'll have a Dewar's on the rocks with two large olives."

Meg sat quietly, but was glancing at Woody in the mirror behind the bar. His bushy messy hair and tortoise shell frame glasses intrigued her. She could tell he was wearing an old shirt that he probably used to wear in high school.

Woody took a sip of his drink while turning to look around. That first sip always made him pucker up. He glanced into the mirror at Meg and said to himself: Hey, she's doesn't look half bad. She's got kind of an Annie Hall look, hat and all. Their eyes meet in the mirror then quickly look away.

Woody turns away from Meg. An older women is seated on his other side. She smiles at eye contact. She has missing lower middle teeth, with two long teeth, sticking up on each side of the gap. He couldn't help but think back to his high school days when he used to kick field goals. Woody nervously takes a sip of his scotch and blurts out to Meg:

"You look good sitting there." (Damn, what a stupid thing to say, he thought)

"Why, thank you." (Damn, what a stupid thing he said, she thought.)

"Ahhhh … This is my first time here. I mean, well, in this place. I usually go down to the circle at the Bar Bill."

Meg has no comment, turns away from him and rolls her eyes back as she looks for more interesting men.

Just then, another man approaches her.

"Hi, sweetie. Your name must be "Sugar Free Honey," because you look so sweet, without the sugar."

Meg turns back toward Woody and says:

"So … I'm Meg. What is your name?

"My name is Woodrow. But you can call me 'Woody.' Do you come here often?"

"No, but today I'm celebrating passing both the real estate exam and a kidney stone."

"Wow, congratulations on such a productive day. I went to my shrink this afternoon and I feel great."

"I heard that a shrink is a waste of money. Most people don't feel any better," said Meg.

"Not for me. I see him three times a week. My appointments are from 2p.m.—4p.m. He's got this long, glove leather couch. He asks me to lie down. By the third question he asks, I'm sound asleep. At 4p.m. he wakes me up. I've got to tell you, I feel great after each visit. I've heard having a kidney stone is very painful. What does it feel like?"

"Well, it feels like someone connects a fishing hook to some steel wire that is connected to the back of a garden tractor. Then the hook is pushed into your abdomen and catches on your kidney. Then, the garden tractor starts up and pulls on the wire for about two hours."

Woody sips his drink and decides to be sure to drink ten glasses of water a day for the rest of his life.

"Do you have a hobby, Meg?"

"Yes, I do, sort of. Actually, I've turned it into a business."

Woody perks up. Finally, a woman of purpose.

"What is your business?"

"I own a mail order plastic flower shop. Instead of real flowers in a gift box, mine are plastic. My plastic roses are a big seller. Since the flowers are plastic, I can offer a lifetime guarantee."

"What do you do, Woody?"

"Wow, what a coincidence. I'm studying Botany at University of Buffalo."

"Cool. We have so much in common," said Meg.

"My buddies and I were going to start a business. It was going to be an economy funeral service."

"Did you have a name for it?"

"Well, at first we liked *Econo-Plant*, but, we finally settled on *Six Feet Deep Cheap*."

"How did you plan on offering services cheap?"

"Well, we planned a funeral parlor, with a beautifully decorated interior. In the parlor would be a really high-end casket and floral arrangements. Throughout the day, different bodies would be displayed in the same casket. We figured we could run ten stiffs through a day."

"How did you bury the bodies?"

"We planned these large Ziploc bags to bury them in."

"Why didn't you go through with the business?" asked Meg.

"I don't know. Why does a pigeon's head bounce back and forth when they walk?"

"Well … I've got to go. I have to return a book to a buddy of mine."

"What's the name of the book, Woody?"

"*The Last Funeral Planning Book You Will Ever Need*. Say, would you like to go out to dinner with me on Friday night? This place has an all you can eat liver and onions special before 5p.m."

"Sure … "

Walking with Jesus

The Disciples learn about Jesus, Heaven, and Hell.

SHORTLY AFTER JESUS HAD FORMED HIS GROUP OF DISCIPLES, they were walking along the Sea of Galilee from Capernaum to Tabgha. The night before they had spent a restful night under a large Kermes Oak tree.

"Rabbi, when we walk to different places we just walk in any direction. We have no map. We seem to just wander."

"Simon Peter, my Father has no map for us. He has asked us to speak with all people in all places. The people along any road or trail deserve to have us talk with them just as much as those who live within a map."

"But, how will we know the way?"

"Way, there is no way, except through me or my Father. We teach from person to person, not town to town."

"What do we say to people? They do not know us?"

Just then, a man was approaching in the other direction with a heavily laden donkey. The donkey is limping and in obvious agony. It's knee is red and swollen. As the group is passing the donkey stopped and looked intently at Jesus.

"Hello, Ariel of Capernaum." Jesus welcomed.

"How do you know my name? I do not know you. Who are you?"

"My name is Jesus of Nazareth. My Father has sent me here to talk with you. My Disciples and I are traveling and speaking to all who will hear us. Ariel, I tell you that I have always known you. I am your warmth on a cold night. I am the quenching when you drink cold water. I am the feel of a knot, which is made taut. You need only ask God to teach you to know and accept me as your Savior. Do this, Ariel, and you will have everlasting life in my Father's Heaven."

Jesus asked Ariel if he could mend the donkey's knee and the man approved. As Jesus softly caressed the donkey's knee, the redness and swelling began to subside and soon was fully healed.

"Ariel, if you believe in me and my Father, so too shall you be healed."

The group continued along the lonely stretch of hot, dusty trail.

"Rabbi, why are we not rallying the people against the Romans? I see the hatred in the soldier's eyes when they look at us."

"Andrew, after the Romans there will be another oppressive group. After them, another. This will continue until all men realize hatred and oppression are not of the Father. We must treat others with respect and dignity. Without this insight, it will always be Man who takes a small neatly wound ball of twine and makes it into a large, bulky, ball of hopelessly tangled twine."

"But Rabbi, they hate us and work us into poor health and old age. They tax us, leaving us with just barely enough to live."

"And so will the one's that will follow the Romans, Simon. You need only the Father."

"Rabbi ... how do we acquire your peace and understanding?"

"Look out into this field of wild flowers. You see the variety, color, and texture of the grasses and flowers. When did you thank God for all he has given you? God has created an endless amount of beauty and unlimited capacity in your life. You must continue to seek. The path will open up to you. I tell you that the Kingdom of Heaven is within you."

"Rabbi, what does this mean? Please tell us. Tell us fully. You have spoken in parables about Heaven. Master, please tell us of Heaven. We do not understand what Heaven is based on your parables."

"If you did not know what a rose is, or any flower, and you did not know what color and texture are, or what a smell is, how could I describe a beautiful rose to you?"

"I speak in parables because, until you enter Heaven, you do not have the capacity to understand the Majesty. I can only give you some reference based on your life and let you form a vision. You see, the Majesty of Heaven cannot be fully described by any comparison in this life."

"Rabbi, please tell us of this vision."

"It is the joy you will experience when you realize that you love all others. There are no faults and differences. It is the joy of giving freely. It is the joy in your stewardship of the earth and all it's creatures. It is the joy of realizing that you are at peace with yourself. You realize that your possessions have little spiritual value and you freely give them to those in need. It is the joy of knowing that your faith has saved you. This joy is endless and freely given to you. The more you seek this joy, the more will be revealed to you. You see, this capacity is within you."

"Rabbi, you make this sound so simple. How do we know when we have found the Kingdom."

"One day, a woman asked her son to sweep and straighten out his father's pottery workshop. She asked him to see her when he had finished so she could inspect. The son went into the shop and moved a few things around then asked his mother to inspect it. The mother told the boy to do a much better job. The boy does, and again asks his mom to inspect. She does and again encourages the boy to be proud of his work. The boy spends a long time in the workshop. He bursts out of the workshop, runs past his mother and down the dusty road in search of his father."

"So too shall you run to the Father when you have found the Kingdom."

"When the Father calls you and you enter Heaven, upon first sight, your legs will buckle, you will fall to your knees and wail with joy."

"But Rabbi, what is Hell like?"

"You cannot comprehend the full depth of Hell without first establishing a loving a relationship with our Heavenly Father. When you do this, it will occur to you exactly what Hell is. If the Devil calls you and you enter Hell, upon first sight, your legs will buckle, you will fall to your knees and wail in agony."

"Come ... we must continue down the path. Many will listen ... but few will hear."

Acknowledgments

I would like to thank my love, Nancy Washburn, for the many hours of poring over every word of this book to ensure my voice came through clearly and accurately.

My thanks to my son, Andrew Lee, for the design of my book cover.

I would also like to thank my old friends, Norman Satanoski, Johnnie Mulvihill (#3), and 'Iron Mike' Ruby (#1), for their historical comments during the development of the book.

CPSIA information can be obtained
at www.ICGtesting.com
Printed in the USA
FFOW02n1910210618
47183146-49861FF